dpInk

Donnaink Publications, L.L.C.

Laughingcleaver Press

Quarantina

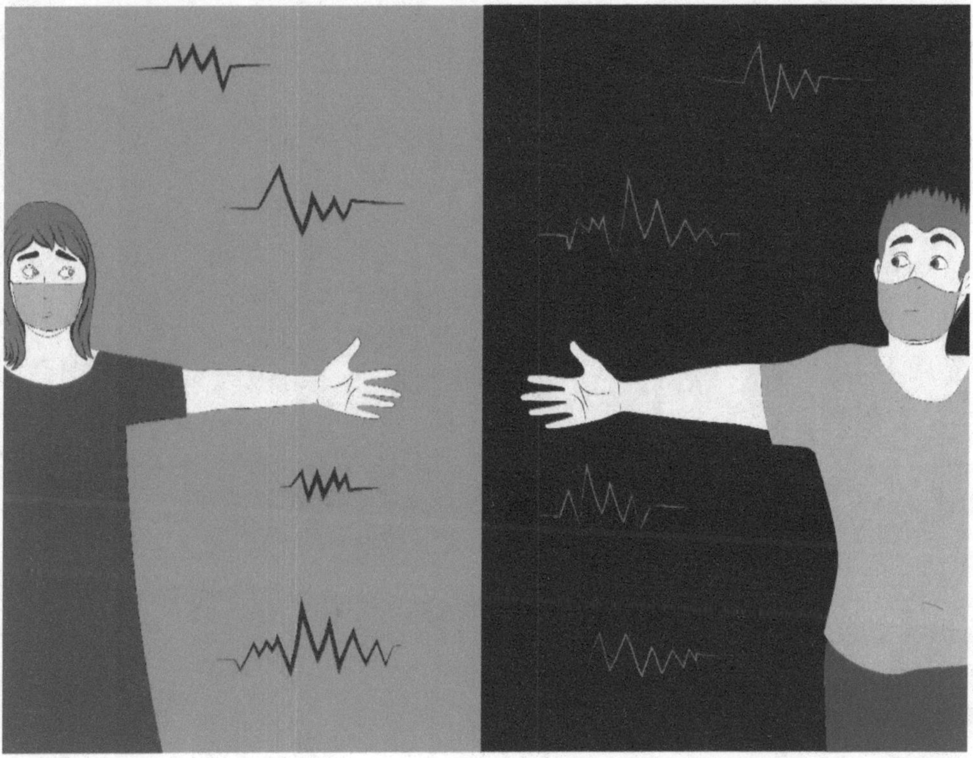

Laughingcleaver Press | DonnaInk Publications, L.L.C.

Laughingcleaver Press
United States of America

Quarantina

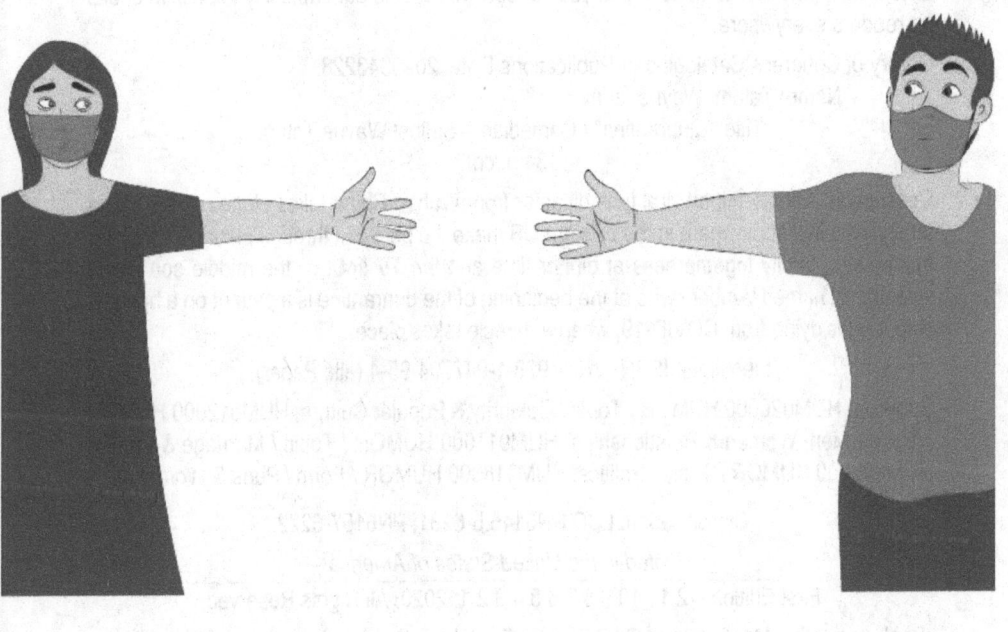

By

WAYNE TATUM

Laughingcleaver Press
An imprint of DonnaInk Publications, L.L.C.
17611 Aquasco Road, Brandywine, MD 20613
Publisher Since 2012

Laughingcleaver Press

Library of Congress Cataloging-in-Publications Data: 2020943228.

Name: Tatum, Wayne, author.

Title: "Quarantina" / Comedian – Satirist Wayne Tatum
134 p. cm.

Description: After a 'minor' viral type disaster from Wuhan China takes place . . . the Kovid family, who live somewhere in the Eastern US make the best of it through planned shopping maneuvers, family togetherness at dinner time and the TV set . . . the middle son has a sweetheart named 'Amber', who at the beginning of the quarantine is a patient on a hospital ship, and is dying from COVID-19, when a miracle takes place.

Identifiers: ISBN – 13 – 978-1-947704-95-4 (alk. Paper).

Subjects: HUM020000 HUMOR / Topic / Celebrity & Popular Culture; HUM012000 HUMOR / Topic / Men, Women & Relationships; HUM011000 HUMOR / Topic / Marriage & Family; HUM006000 HUMOR / Topic / Politics; HUM018000 HUMOR / Form / Puns & Wordplay.

Classification: LCC PN6146.5-6231; PN6157-6222.

Printed in the United States of America

Book design by: Ms. Donna L. Quesinberry, Founder & President, DonnaInk Publications.

Book illustrations by: Riea Naskar, M.A. English University of Calcutta, India.

DonnaInk Publications, L.L.C.
17611 Aquasco Road, Brandywine, MD 20613
www.donnaink.shop

QUARANTINA

OTHER BOOKS BY WAYNE TATUM

Illustrated Tales for the Easily Entertained

DEDICATION

This story is dedicated to all who worked hard to fight this thing from the beginning, the poor folk who managed to hang on through the ensuing shutdown, and my wife Leidiane, whose job was also put on hold, allowing us to share more hours of our day, together, than we have been able to do in the past twenty years.

TABLE OF CONTENTS

iNTRODUCTiON

In the cold silence of the Chinese winter, late 2019, a deadly virus is released into the population of the City of Wuhan from a laboratory located within its borders. No mention of the release of the disease is made by the Chinese government.

Some of the more vigilant world governments, after hearing about a pneumonia breakout of unknown cause in Wuhan City from the World Health Organization (WHO) (eventually named COVID-19, aka 'The Wuhan Virus'; an easily-spread SARS-type disease) managed to lessen effects of the outbreak by quarantining citizens to stop the looming pandemic, which was stated to be worse than the Spanish flu of 1917.

The Chinese government first blamed American soldiers. Then, they blamed the Pangolin, a rare, armored creature resembling an Armadillo. Eventually, the blame shifted to an escaped bat that ended up in an outdoor Wuhan meat market, not known for cleanliness or sanitary environment (Asian meat markets, that is).

Rumors leak referencing lab vials and a clumsy technician, a Harvard professor linked to the laboratory with political ties and 'bad actor' tendencies. One or more US universities may have supplied money to the lab under the title of 'Bat-human virus transmission.'

Nevertheless, economies of many nations suffer because of protective quarantining for their respective populace. Lawsuits against the Chinese government continue to grow in number due to deaths resulting from the insidious man-created scourge.

The question remains among more inquisitive and possibly paranoid minds around the globe as to whether or not the outbreak was purposeful, as in 'malice of forethought,' and what that purpose could possibly be.

Let's hope answers to these questions come soon, and SOMEONE is fired from their laboratory job with extreme prejudice, or at the very least, their mistake results in a very bad mark upon their resume, with extreme measures to follow.

ACKNOWLEDGEMENT

Special thanks to my friends and interested folks who may have read my soap opera version on a weekly basis by way of WordPress, LinkedIn, or my publisher-sponsored Facebook Fan Page (https://www.facebook.com/authorwaynetatum).

I hope whoever reads this romantic soap opera parody, gets a real kick out of it.

Stay safe!

PROLOGUE

We see and hear a large gong being struck, causing a bat of somewhat considerable size to fly out from behind it, escaping its enclosed environment through a white bio-lab door.

The creature zooms through a Chinese meat market, then dramatically soars up into the sky. It morphing from a dark brown color to red-green as a caduceus appears causing the oddly radar-free avian mammal to splatter into it. And as the once bitty-beastie slowly oozes down the symbol of hope, two ghostly Chinese ancients at each end bow with hands together and fingers pointed upward at chest level . . . this is when we hear the title spoken in a soothing female voice:

"Quarantina"

QUARANTINA

EPIGRAPH

Love does not delight in evil but rejoices with the truth. It always protects, always trusts, always hopes, always perseveres.

1 Corinthians 13:6

Quarantina

CHAPTER ONE

Mainland China - a Chinese army officer in an undisclosed bunker located near an airport and commercial harbor is interrogating a female scientist concerning comments she made on the national television station a few days earlier concerning a missing lab vial and one particular test animal. She tells him the truth and refuses to retract statements about what she revealed and threatens to go to the worldwide press to expose the nature and history of the biological war department in the City of Wuhan. Swiftly, she is taken away, never to be heard from again. The army officer slowly walks outside the bunker. He takes a deep breath and ponders the future while viewing international flights taking off for various destinations, with keen, but sad interest in an on-boarding cruise ship full of excited passengers.

A LITTLE DAMAGE CONTROL
AND AS LITTLE AS POSSIBLE

Mainland China, two months later - the virus is killing many Chinese citizens, but their government refuses to acknowledge it to the world press - all is fine in the Land of the Dragon!

At a press conference, the Chinese government admits there is a 'slight problem,' blaming everything and everybody but themselves.

Eventually, it is figured out the 'slight problem' is the accidental (or possibly intentional) release of an unknown virus that appeared in the City of Wuhan by way of an animal; a SARS mutation potentially from a busted lab vial, or perhaps, a natural occurrence stemming from a wet meat market. The goal was to figure out when to contain that city by way of a secretly forced quarantine, just long enough to calm everybody down until the incident can be forgotten overseas. Chinese leadership offer strained smiles for the camera, which frightens more people than it appeases.

MEANWHILE
ON THE OTHER SIDE OF THE WORLD

Eastern United States - an American family named, Kovid, lay around their living room, watching the news. They perk up about any news from Wuhan, becoming especially attentive when stories about cruise ships and international flights carrying diseased passengers aired. They watched as the President of the United States spoke for the first time about the illness that began in the City of Wuhan. The broadcast is displayed in split screen, showing those who love the President and those who do not. The middle Kovid son, Ripp, who is sixteen, five-foot ten, dark haired, sensitive, handsome, and athletic, attempts to change the channel when his parents snapped at him, causing him to change it back. The news shifted to all incoming passenger flights and ships being quarantined for fourteen days, causing the boys to sit up. The other sons, Ray, a five-foot nine scholarly-sounding, light brown-haired and clean-cut squire of seventeen, and Ryk, a short tow-headed bulldog of thirteen, looked toward each other, then at Ripp.

"Hey Ripp?" asked Ray, "Wasn't Amber's family coming back from their vacation in China on a cruise ship?"

"Shut up Ray!" replied Ripp not wanting his parents to know about his school life.

"Who is Amber?" his Dad inquires.

"She's Ripp's sweetheart," replied Ray.

"Ray, can you please just stop – " started Ripp, when Ryk joins in with, "Ripp has a girlfriend . . . Ripp has a girlfriend," causing Ripp to jump Ryk in mock-combat wielding a couch pillow.

"Grow up Ryk, the guy is sixteen after all," continued Ray.

Meanwhile, their mother, who wasn't enjoying watching her furniture being slowly and irreparably damaged, decided to join in the conversation. "Boys knock it off," she remonstrates. "Ripp, it is perfectly normal for a sixteen-year-old boy to believe he's in love with a proper, decent-type, girl."

"Yeah . . . especially when they look like Amber!" chided Ryk, causing on more round of brother Ripp's 'shut up' chorus ending with,

"I'm going to bed. Good night, all."

Mom spoke back, loudly, "Ripp, it is perfectly normal - " but he cuts her off mid-sentence.

"Good NIGHT, Mom," and closed his bedroom door.

Ray walked up to their mother and said, "She's really cute Mom, you know, for a rah-rah nerdy girl."

"Yeah Mom," Ryk agreed, "Amber's hot - just like you probably were when you met dad."

"Ryk!" she cried in comedic shock. Ray jumped in to protect their mother's dignity. "Mom wasn't HOT, Ryk," he riposted. "Man, are you sick! Hey, that rhymes."

"So, Dad married Mom out of pity?" Ryk asked.

"Oh boy," she groused.

At this point, their father stood up and orated all the glories and failures of life and love in marriage.

"Guys, we were young once and your MOTHER was and still is 'very' beautiful," he declared.

"Anything you say Dad. We believe you," concurred Ray, winking at his mom.

"What??!!" she retorted, causing Ray to jump up off of the couch to hug her adding. "Just kidding, Mom. You are beautiful."

"Thank you," she replied.

At this point, Dad shifted gears, returning to the original subject of interest. "Now, what about this girl, Amber?" he asked, "Do you think she's on a cruise liner from China?"

"I don't know, dad," Ray responded. "All I know is she was touring cities in China with her family and a Pacific cruise is the way back she spoke about."

Pondering Ray's response, Dad replied, "I see. Well, we shouldn't be too worried guys. Hopefully, they'll stop the disease in its tracks before it ever has a chance to get to her or us."

"Don't forget to turn the lights out after you go to bed, kids. Good night!" added Mom.

Ray and Ryk, looked at their parents as they left the room and when they were out of sight, they simultaneously exclaimed, "Movie time!"

From her bedroom door, Mom responded, "Keep the sound down tonight!"

After dutifully replying, "Yes, mom," Ray whispered to Ryk, "Turn it back UP."

"BOYS," warned Dad.

"Ok! Rats," groaned Ryk. as Ray smiled.

A REAL GEM
OF AN IMPORT

There is a thrift store in the Kovid family's town, sometimes run, but mostly overrun by Daman, a bossy twenty-five-year old international who goes by the name, Tom, and he 'works' with otherwise decent folk who tend to be their local customers. This particular store operates on cash provided by those same local customers who obtain items at low costs by way of donations from other locals. These items are normally used or worn. The actual store manager's name is, Bitsy, but she is out this day. Her backup is, Hildy, a tall, thoughtful white-haired woman who is very old and somewhat slow, now resting comfortably in Bitsy's office at the rear of the establishment.

Because of this unique situation, Tom struts around the main floor looking for customers to rush to purchase, causing some to buy items that they don't even want. One unassuming, well-meaning customer meekly approached the checkout counter to discuss a donation.

"How may I help you?" asked the checkout line girl.

"Yes. I'd like to donate these quad speakers," replied the customer.

"Let me see if . . . " the checkout girl began, when Tom rudely cut in . . .

"I will take it from here. Sir, we do not take partial or incomplete donations."

"Are you in charge of donations?" inquired the customer.

"I said, we do not take partial donations," stated the brusque store representative.

"Who exactly is in charge of donations here?" asked the rebuffed customer. "May I please speak with the person in charge?"

Ignoring the customer's honest request for fair treatment, and being that Tom was a master in the crude art of a haggle in any and every situation, he replied, "You are speaking with ME, now. And we do not take – " as the beaten customer sighs, "Partial donations." Tom continued his grand denial of service by pointing out to the customer, "We have a trash receptacle out back if you wish to throw them away, which is all they are worth here."

The customer mumbled, "Fine, sheesh," and exited the store.

Hildy, had overheard part of the exchange, though, and calmly confronted Tom concerning his treatment of customers. "This is the fourth donor you have sent away this week," she points out. "Of COURSE, we would have taken his items, we're not an auction house for rich clientele. We accept donations of all kinds!"

Tom replied to her, using an amazing and well-honed baffle-the-biddy-techno-jargon performance that never seemed to fail. "Hildy, I know speakers, and I must tell you that they were a blown, incomplete set, exhibiting smoke marks on the back panels compounded with the smell of burnt wires! I am an expert, and you should trust me on this."

But Hildy was, at times, wise to con artists, and Tom left her an opening. "May I see them?" she innocently asked.

"See what?" Tom inquired in like fashion.

"The speakers you took from him," she replied.

"It's too late. They are already in the trash bin," he finalized. "You must take my word for this, Hildy. Do not worry about those things, it is already over and done. I am glad to have performed this duty for you."

The elderly woman shook her head and walked away.

Successful once more, Tom *the International* continued to go about the store harassing customers into purchasing items they did not need or desire. Meanwhile, a very old analogue television set near the front desk was on, allowing all who cared to see and hear the President of the United States describing steps to deal with the newly titled, 'Wuhan Virus.' Tom scoffed and derided him a bit, then went about his business after turning the channel to a chair-throwing mayhem show. Later that evening, he climbed into the lone, green trash dumpster that sat behind the store and in seconds, four speakers went flying over the top. Tom stuck his head out, looked around, and then merrily skittered out, constantly looking behind him to make sure no one was watching.

GREETINGS WITH APOLOGIES
NON-HOARDERS OF AMERICA

A few days after Ripp's parents heard about his girlfriend, Amber, and her potential virus-ridden voyage from China, the US government re-names the Wuhan Virus, the Wuhan Coronavirus or 'COVID-19.' The family was taken aback, but they all agreed not to make a big fuss over it. *That is what their friends and coworkers were going to do.*

Meanwhile . . . a long-term quarantine had been put into place by the federal and state governments. For teens and college-aged kids, not to mention middle-aged bar hounds and goodtime Charlies, that meant no dating, parties, work, or outings other than for necessities. It was at this time tissue paper hoarding rose dramatically. Dad and Mom worked out a tissue paper capture scheme involving all family members, two cars and an early morning wake up call, as other local households were finding some mild success at the large family tissue game using this very same tactic.

Mom, Dad and Ryk took turns snagging single bags of tissue at a warehouse store while Grandpa and Ray took turns doing the same at another mega-store. Sadly, however, while Grandpa spent a lot of precious time trying to find items while avoiding drooling children and ghost shopping carts, not to mention one human accident, where he ran smack into a sniffling, hacking ill person of possible disease origin.

"Oh NO," he blurted out in final defeat, only using a slightly different, but very significant variation of an old familiar oath.

The fear of having caught the deadly Wuhan virus was now upon him.

MOPEY LOVE

Ripp was the only Kovid not enlisted for the tissue hunt. He told his parents he wasn't up to the shopping spree, and even after a few attempts at telling him going out would do him some good, and one mild threat to his future freedom, they figured that a mopey teen would be a useless teen. Ripp spent the entire morning attempting to contact Amber, who was still aboard the plagued cruise.

THE YOUNG AND THE RECKLESS

That evening, Mom complained about everything, snapped at everyone, and appeasement wasn't possible, so to escape her line of fire, Ray and Ryk headed to the basement for safety. As the two lads looked for something to do that didn't involve boards or dice, they found an old karaoke machine with mic and TV hookup--CDs included.

After trying a few rap numbers and some oldies bought by Mom and Dad, their musical revue devolved into a belching contest, further disgraced by reverb and bass overtones. It was at this time Grandpa entered the room to find out what they were up to. The boys encouraged him to give it a try.

"I'm too old for this nonsense," he replied.

But the boys had heard stories about their grandfather in the old days and weren't having it.

"C'mon Grandpa," coaxed Ray. "Show us how you did it in the service!"

"Yeah," agreed Ryk, "C'mon Gramps, cut loose!"

The old man thought about looking dignified, acting his age, putting the past behind. But those were just elderly gentleman excuses, and this aged but proud fellow wasn't ready to give up just yet, he who once was the greatest human foghorn and bullfrog impressionist in uniform, according to his surviving buddies.

"Give me that thing," he gruffly demanded grabbing the microphone out of Ray's hand.

"Go, Grandpa!" shouted the boys.

The old man sets himself for action, tried to burp, but failed to deliver.

"So, Grandpa . . . is that all you got?" Ray asked.

"Time to retire." Added Ryk, displaying a mock-sorrowful expression on his face.

Grandpa stared at his two hecklers, gritted his false teeth, and squared himself into a sumo wrestling position. He strained, and strained away, but no belch appeared, even as the boys cheered and mocked. But suddenly, Grandpa emitted a loud and very unnatural sound. His face turned pale. The boys looked at him, then to each other.

After a few long moments, Grandpa spoke in a whisper.

"What did you say?" asked Ryk.

"It sounded like he said he doesn't feel so well," answered Ray.

Grandpa managed to nod his head, even while bent over the karaoke machine and in much discomfort.

ORDERS FROM HQ

The next morning, Mom Kovid had Ray and Ryk lined up in the basement. Grandpa had been driven to the emergency room by Dad the night of the disaster. The karaoke machine and microphone were defiled beyond repair, plus the boys lost their basement privileges for a week, even during a quarantine that was already causing cabin fever.

The potentially volcanic situation made absolutely no imprint on Commandant Mom. "You two are going to get rid of this infernal machine AFTER you completely scour this part of the room. WASH Grandpa's shirt and disinfect the entire karaoke set BEFORE you get rid of it. And . . . no more crude contests. Is that CLEAR?" she demanded.

Ryk and Ray gave their well-rehearsed, correct, and penitent floor-staring reply, "Yes ma'am."

Their mother gazed at them both, then hurried out of the room and up the stairs.

Ryk waited a moment, looked over at Ray and said, "Man, GP really got sick in a hurry."

"Yeah, the timing was incredible," Ray replied. "Anyway, let's make sure Mom doesn't have a reason to lay into us a second time. So, I'll get the car and you clean. Then, we need to find some kind of donation place."

Surprised and slightly incensed over Ray's work detail breakout, Ryk asked, "Why should I clean? You were here too!"

"Hey, I wasn't the one who told him to 'cut loose,'" Ray calmly replied. "Your fault, you clean. Very fair and simple. Get me?"

"Sooner than you think," answered Ryk in looming-threat brother-style code.

"Good man," noted Ray as he headed up the stairs. "See you soon."

THE SECRET SOCIETY OF DADS

Ripp had tried over and over to contact Amber. The news broadcast around the world was that the Coronavirus was a certain death sentence if contracted, and any ship out of China would soon become a floating mortuary. Even so, Ripp kept dialing, and on his first try that morning, the phone was picked up and a male voice answered.

"Hello."

"Uh, yessir, may I speak with Amber?" asked Ripp, still in a bit of shock and surprise.

"Who IS this?" demanded the man.

Ripp straightened his posture a bit, and replied, "Sir, I am a school friend of Amber's - may I speak with her, please?"

But the man at the other end was not quite satisfied with the boy's reply and rephrased his question: "Do you have a name?"

Ripp replied, "My name is Ripp, er, ah, Ripley, sir."

"Ripley WHO?" inquired the mystery voice.

"Kovid," replied Ripp.

"Do you think that's funny, son?" the man asked, as if it were an interrogation. "Amber is in intensive care and you're making a joke of it?"

Ripp received the answer he feared but continued on. "Sir, my last name is Kovid, with a 'K,'" he replied.

The man at the other end wasn't so sure. "Son if you're playing games with me, I swear . . . "

Ripp knew this sort of problem with his last name could come up during the quarantine, so he laid his entire case out for the inquisitive older person. "Sir," he stated, "We attend the same school and I would never do ANYTHING to hurt Amber. Ask her, she'll tell you my last name is really Kovid!"

The man at the other end paused, then asked, "Are either of your parents home? I'd like to speak with one of them."

"Oh boy," thought Ripp as he called out, "DAAAAADDDDD!"

His father rushed to the doorway and asked, "What? What's the problem?"

Ripp replied, "Phone call for you."

His father was relieved, but a bit peeved at having to rush to a non-emergency. He stared at Ripp while answering the phone. "Hello, Rod Kovid here."

The voice at the other end replied, "Yes this is Amber's father. Your son called here looking for my daughter. And your last name really is . . . Kovid?"

"YES, Amber's Father," Dad reiterated, "That's Kovid with a 'K,' and NO, it is not a joke. I prefer the 'Wuhan Virus' if you'd like to know, but with government anagrams, what can you do?"

Slightly relieved, but still officious, Amber's father replied, "Just checking and so sorry about your last name. I wish you all the best."

"Great, here's my son" Dad said while handing the phone back to Ripp, adding, "Please warn us if you intend to marry that girl someday. We might have a slight problem on the invitations, 'Father of the groom, Rodney Kovid. Father of the bride, Amber's Father.' Mull that over some, will you?" After Rod Kovid delivered the fatherly benediction to his son, he left the room shaking his head.

Ripp continued on, asking Amber's father once more, "Sir, may I please speak with her?"

Amber's father seemed much more understanding this time around. "Son, she can barely speak right now, and it's been very tough for all of us. I will tell her you called. Okay?"

The young Kovid is encouraged by the answer and pressed once more. "Yessir, but can you also tell her . . . " but Amber's father hung up the phone without hearing Ripp's sincere plea.

"Oh rats . . . " mumbled Ripp as he laid the phone down.

"Mull it over!" warned Dad, as he listened in from the living room.

It seemed to Ripp, somewhere in the distance was the sound of an Asian gong.

CHAPTER TWO

PUTTING THE BEST

TO THE TEST

After Ryk's morning of cleaning and being somewhat grossed out, he and brother Ray drove over to a donation center they were lucky enough to find close to home. Ryk's cleaning job on the karaoke set was seemingly adequate but rushed. Ray grabbed the box of song CDs, while Ryk carried the still somewhat odiferous karaoke machine and microphone. Upon entering the store, they rushed over to the bemasked and rubber-gloved cashier to ask about donations. The cashier attempted to call Bitsy, the manager, to see the items when Tom *the International* magically appeared and plunged the pushbutton telephone switch hook down, canceling the call between the startled young cashier and unknowing manager Bitsy.

"How may I be of service to you?" asked Tom.

Ryk jumped right in, replying, "Yeah! We wanna get rid of this . . . "

At this point, Ray uses one arm to politely push Ryk away from the counter as he, himself, moved toward Tom and politely mentioned, "What my brother MEANT to say was that we wish to donate this barely used, highly rated family fun center for cash or trade."

Tom removed all expression from his face while gearing up with rude disregard of these amateurish children, and forcefully stated, "We absolutely do NOT give cash or trade. In FACT, we do not accept incomplete electronic devices. NOR do we accept cheap or worn out music systems. You must either take it with you or you can throw it out back in the dumpster. It is unacceptable in its current condition."

Ryk had heard enough at this point from the disrespectful salesman and attempted to rush past Ray to get at him.

"Oh YEAH?" demanded Ryk, "What's wrong with it?"

Ray moved Ryk behind him and politely asked the salesman, "May I inquire what your dilatory observations of this superb, one-of-a-kind, portable, rocking beast-box of woofers and tweeters are that would cause you to dismiss it in such a cavalier fashion?"

"Yeah, what's wrong with it?" repeated Ryk.

Ray tried to quiet Ryk down in order for his own smooth methodology to work, but Tom didn't take the bait.

"I will TELL you what is wrong with it," answered the churlish salesman. "This sound device is old and third rate, used up, the plug has no ground and is therefore, unsafe. The CD player is not up-to-date, the corded microphone is analogue and not a cordless digital type, the housing is faded, the dials are close to cracking, and I can go on and on. It is useless for this place of business; it has no retail value. So, to save everyone much more useless trouble, you should expedite it quickly from here before someone sees it and decides to shop elsewhere."

"You're FULL of it!" cried Ryk.

Ray placed his hand on Ryk's shoulder and used the kindness tactic once more. "Is there someone ELSE in this fine establishment I might have the pleasure of speaking with?"

"You are speaking with ME now," declared the brusque salesman. "Please remove that thing from here. It is unsafe and should be considered a fire hazard."

Ryk tried to jump at Tom, but Ray stopped him, and as he did, he also noticed something on the microphone from the night before.

"Fine, no problem then," agreed Ray, while Ryk stared at him incredulously. "May I ask your name, again?"

Tom was dumbfounded by the boy's stupidity. "Can't you read my name tag?" he asked.

"Oh yes," replied Ray. "I just thought you were kidding. Sorry, TOM."

Exiting the store, karaoke machine and extras in hand, Ray sauntered to the back of the building and pretended to toss the system into the dumpster as Ryk caught up to him.

"What are you DOING?" cried Ryk.

Ray put his arm around Ryk's shoulder and whispered, "You didn't clean it very well - I could smell it, even inside that moldy old store!"

"So why didn't you toss it?" Ryk wanted to know.

"I just wanted to see what that guy actually does with it," Ray replied.

Ryk retorted, "That could be all day!"

"I don't think so," said Ray. "It's a great system and he knows it."

Ray returned to the store to tell Tom the dumpster is locked and that he placed the karaoke set in front of it. Meanwhile, Ryk waited by the car, frustrated, and completely baffled.

"We do not lock the dumpster! It is not possible!" shouted Tom.

"Well," continued Ray, "it appears someone DID. Sorry to have wasted your valuable time. See ya!"

Tom is not used to being treated in this fashion. "Come back here and properly remove that useless pile of hoodoo from the front of our dumpster!" he shouted.

Ray met Ryk at the car, gets in and swiftly drove off to a nearby warehouse within viewing range of the dumpster. Tom, meanwhile, was still screaming at them from the front door of the building, not knowing where they had gone.

"I will call to the police!" he shrieked.

Defeated for the first time since his primitive early childhood – something to do with a serpent - Tom walked to the rear of the building to check the dumpster and found it was indeed unlocked as he stated, causing him to grow more and more irate. But before he tossed the karaoke system away, he noticed the battery power switch on the front of the face plate and flipped it on. He tried out the microphone. The karaoke set was actually quite good. He placed the entire system behind the dumpster for later retrieval. His nasty demeanor changed to a mild disdain of customers as he returned to the store while constantly looking behind him for observers and witnesses.

Ray and Ryk did witness it in fact, from inside their car near a warehouse, out of sight from the store.

"Told ya," said Ray as Ryk looked on, rightly awed by his brother's insight.

OLD MEN
OLD TRICKS

Grandpa rested quietly in the local hospital emergency room awaiting test results. Mom and Dad Kovid arrived in time to hear the doctor tell Grandpa he has a virus - but, fortunately, not the Corona version, which brought much relief to the entire family. But the doctor also wished to retest him before sending him home.

"We don't have a lot of space in here," said the doctor, "but there will be some temporary rooms opening up soon. Just as a precaution. Any questions? Stay well."

After the doctor left them to see other patients, Grandpa said, "I tried staying well and I ended up here, instead! Anyway, you folks go on home and get some rest. I'll be just fine unless the television dies on me."

"We'll be by later, dad," said Mom.

"Hang in there, Pops. Try not to chase the nurses around too much, huh?" jested Dad.

"I won't promise anything," replied the old man. "Depends how bored I get. Get on home, you two." But after his daughter and son-in-law left, Grandpa's seeming 'devil-may-care' attitude swiftly changed, revealing his inner turmoil and concern over COVID-19 updates on the TV.

It is at this time; a middle-aged nurse entered the room wearing a mask and plastic gloves. While checking Grandpa's pulse, blood pressure and temperature, he asked, "Will I live?"

"As long as you don't try to chase me around the hospital all day," she replied.

Grandpa smiled and confessed all, saying "You heard that, did you? Well, I am lucky if I can walk two steps, today. But maybe tomorrow, so watch out!"

"Oh, I'm sure you're stronger than that! So, what brought you in here last night?" she asked.

Grandpa tried to hide most of his embarrassing predicament earlier caused by boorish behavior, but he managed to get away with it by saying "Well, if you must know, I was horsing around with my grandsons when I managed to redesign the rug and entertainment system at the same time."

"You had a seizure?" inquired the nurse.

Grandpa grimaced in memory of that night and replied, "My stomach sure did! I became awfully ill at a most inopportune moment."

"Poor old entertainment system," bemoaned the nurse.

"Alas," recited Grandpa.

The nurse looked at him, and noted, "Well, despite your archaic language skills, you sound like a fun person to be around."

"Maybe we could horse around singing karaoke sometime," he mentioned in jest, but also as an offer.

The nurse is on to him and replied, "I will if my entertainment system needs to be redecorated."

"Grrrrr," growled the old man, causing his upper denture to fall out. "Uh, could you please retrieve those for me?" he asked.

The nurse stared at him quizzically while raising her eyebrow, then she smiled at him after grabbing the fallen denture. "A real fun person to be around, yes indeed," the nurse reiterated as if she were already prepared to pick up after him on a daily basis.

"You'll never get bored," promised the old man.

"I'll just bet I won't," agreed the nurse.

Grandpa was really enjoying this exchange and didn't wish for it to end.

"Then you can start by calling me Pops" he declared. "And, you are?"

"Your nurse. Call me if you need me," she replied, and then exited the room.

"Yeahhh," intoned Grandpa, half-heartedly. But before he sunk back into his earlier somber mood, the nurse returned.

"Nancy," she stated.

"What?" Grandpa asked, not believing his old ears.

The nurse lowered her mask just long enough to say to him, "That's my name. Call if you need me."

Then she exited the room for the second time.

Grandpa thought about that statement, and how she went about saying it. Now, with a grin on his face and resting his head on a pillow, he intoned once again, and with feeling, "Yeeahhh!"

THE GROOVY VISCERAL
SOUND SYSTEM RIDES AGAIN

On the evening of that same day, Daman, aka Tom, is at home with his extended family. After a large supper, they rejoined in his townhome living room for entertainment. He surprised his cousin, Reg, with the karaoke system.

"So, what do you think of my latest acquisition?" asked Tom.

Reg thinks about it but is a bit uneasy at the same time. "I think," he started, "I think it looks great, but – "

Tom felt a bit insulted by this, but he decided to give Reg his one minute of glory.

"What?" he asked. "What is the problem?"

Reg sniffed, put one hand on his hip, and used his other hand to cradle his chin. "Hmmmm," he started, "It smells."

"Like WHAT?" demanded Tom. "Like WHAT?"

"It smells," replied Reg carefully, not wishing to upset his cousin, "It smells like a sick old man."

Tom, at that point, realized his cousin had not spent enough time in the holy places of their old country.

Tom put his arm around Reg and smiled up at the ceiling. "It reminds me of our most blessed river," he sighs.

"Yah well, maybe you're right," answered Reg as he sniffs the dubious odor again.

"Come," said Tom, "Enough time wasted. Get everybody together. Brides-to-Be on one side, Grooms-to-Be on the other."

Tom looked around and whispered to himself, "I finally have a use for this old karaoke CD from home."

Dancers in position, the room was filled with sitar and rhythm instruments from the CD. Women began performing choreographed steps. A very nasal sounding woman's voice on the CD whined on, followed by Tom singing the male solo.

*(NOTE: Song is deciphered phonetically
for English speaking readers.)*

TOM:

"WEEeeeiiee, yes, my DAR-a-LINGG!"

WOMAN:

"Dar-a-ling - mi zeegna beenga moolah beni dingi du mush cakes?"

TOM:

"WEEeeiee, a mush cake beenga, yes my dar-a-lingg!"

WOMAN:

"Dar-a-ling - a beena deenga doolum dagoosh sweetie beatie?"

TOM:

"WEEeeiieee, a sweetie beetie beenga, bi du, yes, my Dar-a-LINGG!"

The men and women danced in sync, respectively, to well-rehearsed choreography as the unseen female singer and Tom continued their duet. But after a few songs, Tom finally noticed what Reg warned him about earlier, plus there was noticeable gunk on the microphone. Tom ran outside, with Reg following to see if he was all right.

Tom made a very unnatural sound, fell behind a bush, and moaned, "I think I need to go to the hospital."

GRANDPA'S INQUISITIVE
NEW ROOMMATE

Hours later, Tom rested quietly in the local hospital emergency room, awaiting test results. Reg arrived just in time to hear the doctor tell Tom he has a virus, but not the Corona version, which brought much relief to them both. But the doctor also wants to retest him before sending him home. It was the same doctor Grandpa had

"We don't have a lot of space in here," said the doctor, "so we would like to double you up with, interestingly enough, an older male patient who happens to have the same virus as you. We are keeping you overnight just as a precaution. Any questions? Stay well."

As the doctor left the room, Reg mustered up enough courage to make his own exit. Looking at Tom attempting to appear humble by practically prostrating himself, he said, "Tom, I am going home now, but I will bring you some reading material later."

Tom looked away from him in disdain and said, "Fine. Leave then."

"But Tom," begged Reg.

"Go!" replied Tom still looking away from Reg.

With much guilt and a display of shame that would match that of a beaten dog, Reg exited the room.

Satisfied with his performance of perpetual personal hurt and future vengeance, Tom noticed the TV was airing the President's COVID-19 task force update message.

"Not HIM . . . Not NOW . . . " he grumbled, but only then, did he take notice of his elderly roommate.

"Would you mind changing the channel?" he managed to ask, while simultaneously displaying some actual form of politeness.

"Why?" asked Grandpa. "What's wrong with him? He's only trying to save our lives, that's all."

"He is prideful and smug," answered Tom, not caring to recognize the fact the same could be said of him.

"And, he darn well oughta be," declared Grandpa. "The man is doing a great job for our country!"

"Humph," griped Tom. "A lot of higgy-diggy."

Grandpa looked over at him and said, "Well, I'm sorry you feel that way. So, what brings you to this side of the hospital?"

"Wha?" mumbled Tom, absentmindedly, still in mid-inner grumble about having to listen to the President.

"Why are you in HERE?" reiterated Grandpa.

"I suddenly became ill while singing karaoke," replied the fractious foreign fellow.

Grandpa was floored by the young man's answer. "Me too!" he crowed.

Tom thought the old man was trying to pull his leg, so he replied "Please do not play games. I am not in the mood."

Grandpa grew a bit serious at this point and answered "Not playing games, son. My grandkids goaded me into belching as loud as I could into a microphone, but my entire innards appeared, instead. Dinner, lunch, and breakfast everywhere. Just awful."

Tom's hackles AND radar went up at the same time. "Wait a minute," he inquired, "what was it the doctor said? That we both have –"

"The SAME VIRUS!" declared Grandpa and Tom, simultaneously.

"How about that?" muttered Grandpa.

Tom asked, "These grandsons, what do they look like?"

"Well, let's see," started Grandpa, "I figure Ray is seventeen, about five nine, wiry build, brown hair, gray eyes, and Ryk is just a stubby feller –"

"A pushy blond-haired brat?" stated Tom in the form of a question.

"You know him?" Grandpa asked.

"I do NOW. Why those dirty, little –" began Tom when all of a sudden:

"*** WAAAAAAWWWNNKK !!!***"

A buzzing alarm blared from the overly loud TV set while Tom continued to curse about Ray and Ryk.

TV ANNOUNCER:

*"THIS IS A TEST OF THE NATIONAL
EMERGENCY ALERT SYSTEM . . . ."*

Tom cursed on in vain as Grandpa tried and failed to lower the TV volume.

"Dadgummit," mumbled Grandpa. "How about this? Naww, dad blast it."

"*** WAAAAAAWWWNNKK !!!***"

"Maybe this one . . . Nope. Well, I'll be - " Grandpa mumbled again.

"*** WAAAAAAWWWNNKK !!!***"

"Dad burn it." said the old man in mild frustration.

Tom's eyes, ears and forehead grew redder with each fail. Maybe, just maybe, this test will finally end, or the old guy may actually do something right. But just when there was a second of silence:

"*** WAAAAAAWWWNNKK !!!***"

"Dad blast it . . . continued Grandpa.

And the TV station continued to replay it.

The National Emergency Alert System was actually in a loop.

"*** WAAAAAAWWWNNKK !!!***"

"Doggonit and drat the dadgum . . . " spurted Grandpa.

"*** WAAAAAAWWWNNKK !!!***"

"Make it STOP!!" screamed Tom.

"Almost got it," said Grandpa, hopefully.

TV ANNOUNCER:

*"THIS IS A TEST OF THE NATIONAL
EMERGENCY ALERT SYSTEM . . . "*

"Ain't got it," murmured the old man, sadly.

"Oh please, please, please, PLEASE," begged Tom.

"*** WAAAAAAWWWNNKK !!!***"

"Aw, smells bells," bemoaned old man.

"*** WAAAAAAWWWNNKK !!!***"

"Dang it . . . " blurted Grandpa. "This is SOME system, eh, Tom? Sure, has me beat!"

But Tom was beyond all human intervention at this time, as he just screamed and bellowed along to the tune of the National Emergency Broadcast System, pillow around his ears, notwithstanding.

"*** WAAAAAAWWWNNKK !!!***"

"Have to admit, it's mighty powerful. Gotta give in to it. I give up! I'll talk! How about you there, Tom?" laughed Grandpa.

TV ANNOUNCER:

> *"THIS IS A TEST OF THE NATIONAL
> EMERGENCY ALERT SYSTEM . . . "*

"Yee hahh!!" Grandpa shouted.

"*** WAAAAAAWWWNNKK !!!***"

"Hot dog! Yessiree!" Grandpa yelled, as a nurse finally showed up to tend to the screaming, poor international.

CHAPTER THREE

BELOVED

AND BELEAGUERED

The President of the United States is seen in hot debate with news reporters at a White House press conference on TV. The poor man might've said, "Hello," to a Dutchman back in January of 2020, and the press corps would be all over him as to the meaning of it. Nothing he says or does seems right to them. The VP takes over for a bit and the press corps suddenly calm down as if hypnotized.

The Kovid family is watching the COVID-19 update from their living room. Dad was incredulous over the treatment of the President. The latest underground story going around is how much money the President is making off the virus. No proof of course, but it keeps dark, hopeless dreams alive. The good news is he does have defenders, even among the meek, but well-kempt.

Dad shook his head during the latter stages of the 'press conference.'

"I can't believe he left a rich, cushy life in real estate for THIS kind of daily torture," he commiserated.

Mom preferred to note the outer man and her final judgement is "Well, he asks for it when he insults people. He just doesn't BEHAVE in a presidential manner."

"Acting 'Presidential' doesn't always get the job done. This guy is more of a super-consultant hired to fix a failing business," declared Dad.

"The best way to get out of classwork is to mention the President. Most of my teachers foam at the mouth when they hear his name!" added Ryk.

Dad Kovid shook his head once more. "Hard to believe," he said, "that the President's last name can't even be mentioned without causing a riot. Strange days we're living in."

Ray and Ripp entered the living room right around the time Dad makes his final point.

"But maybe not as strange as THIS, Dad. We were watching ads for a crazy movie in Ripp's room just now."

ANNOUNCER ON TV:

> *Tonight's movie: an end-time cult hidden deep in an*
> *Appalachian hollow is discovered by an unwitting*
> *news reporter, who soon becomes their prisoner in*
> *this nineteen seventies classic:*

APOCKYPLEX!

"And, that is my cue to hit the sack. Good night all," Dad replied.

"Those seventies hairdos, alone, are enough to keep me away," mentioned Mom. "Goodnight boys."

"Goodnight," answered the boys in unison.

"Now let's see how weird this movie gets," said Ray, as the other brothers looked on in anticipation of something quite whack.

The movie begins with mist rising from the pale green grass at dawn in the hills. Off-key singing is heard from an old white wooden structure, while ancient, cracked steps lead up into what appears to be a one-room church, where a service is proceeding. The small congregation is filled with wan, poorly dressed, hollow-faced men and women. The leader looks like an old eagle in a baggy striped suit and thin tie.

LEADER'S VOICE:

"We done see'd the light and escaped the evil world."

CONGREGATION:

"Amee-yin!"

LEADER:

"And now, as we, the righteous do pause and ponder with fearful trembulation and shaking hearts, that which is on the world's judgement awaits, as we, the faithful, do trust while they indeed git thars, which they have rightly arned because of thar meeny turble see-yins."

CONGREGATION:

"That's right, amee-yin!"

LEADER:

"Let them that hath sewn the wee-yind reap the whirl wee-yind!"

CONGREGATION:

"Yassir! That's right, the whirl wee-yind."

LEADER:

"They WEEL indaid REAP with thar howlin desires and yearnins, say it now with me,"

LEADER AND CONGREGATION TOGETHER:

"The APAWKEE-PLAY-EX!"

Mercifully, there was a commercial at this point of the film.

Ripp tried to make some modern-day sense out of what he had just seen. "Shouldn't that be pronounced 'APOCALYPSE?'" he asked.

Ray also had his misgivings but explained his view as a movie critic or insider might. "I feel the director wished for his audience to believe the rustic nuances and dialect of the intended populace portrayed," he intimated.

"What?" asked Ryk.

Ripp tried to dumb it down a bit for him. "This movie is what the screen writers thought hillbillies really sounded like," he stated.

"Ah," replied Ryk.

Ray had one more interesting observation. "I can't get over how thin the women were back then."

"Yeah," Ryk agreed. "They look like the women in Grandpa's high school yearbook! What was his girlfriend's name, Weasel Mae somebody or something like that?"

"Willa Mae, you mean?" asked Ray.

Ripp seemed to know this one. "Yeah, and she had a real scarecrowy disease kind of last name. Sounded like hoop."

"Whoop?" asked Ryk.

"Nah," said Ripp. "It was more like Coop, Roop, Whoop, Whooper, Whooping."

"Whooping cough!" declared Ryk.

"Croup, Willa Mae Croup," answered Ray.

"We were close," said Ryk. "Anyway, she'd fit right in with those people."

"Maybe so," concurred Ray. "People pay a lot of money to look that way nowadays."

"Too bad we can't send some of the kids from our school over there," noted Ripp.

Ray looked at Ripp, closely, and smiled.

"Everyone except Amber, you mean, right?" he asked.

"Shut up, Ray," replied Ripp.

"Hey Ripp," asked Ryk, "do you think Amber looks like one of those starving girls in the movie, now, because of the virus?"

Ripp punched Ryk in the arm, and wordlessly headed to his room.

"Where are you going, Ripp?" Ray asked. "The movie will be back on soon."

Ripp replied "I need some privacy."

"Going to cry over Amber again?" teased Ryk.

"Ryk is right for once, Ripley!" goaded Ray. "Show some dignity, man!"

Ryk joined in, declaring "Hey, Ripp, the movie's back on!"

The TV movie congregation is now dancing in a frenzy and gyrating to fiddle and mandolin, one young man even performs a back flip. It was at THAT point when one of the leaders pulled something out of a box.

It wriggled.

It hissed.

It appeared to be venomous.

"Ripp," declared Ray, "they're using snakes!"

Then Ray spoke under his breath in awe: "I've never seen THIS before."

The congregation continues to gyrate in a frenzied manner, as one brave young lady from the congregation reached into a box to pull out a viper, stares it down and then dances hypnotically with it for a long time.

Ray's eyes were transfixed on the screen. "Ripp," he implored "you REALLY need to see this."

"Yeah," agreed Ryk. "The snake is bigger than she is!"

Ray was obsessed with the girl. "Man, is she - " he started, when the snake suddenly gives the young lady a vicious bite, and she falls to the wooden floor in a cold sweat.

"Dead," stated Ray and Ryk in one accord.

Back to his senses, Ray said clearly, "Never mind Ripp, you didn't miss anything! Go agonize over Amber."

Meanwhile, the cult leader furiously grabs the viper from the cold hand of the young lady and throws it back into the box from which it came.

"Oh, maaannn," gasped Ray and Ryk.

The silent congregation looks up at the leader as he looks down upon the departed young lady.

LEADER:

"That a-happened tuh har because she was a-hidin' SECRET SEE-YIN," he declared.

CONGREGTION:

"A-MEE-yin!" cries the congregation.

Ray and Ryk reaffirmed their self-guilt and general awe with one final cry of "Maaaannnnn!"

Mom is still awake and scolded them, saying "Boys, keep it down! We're bringing your grandfather home tomorrow, so Dad and I need to get up early! Good night!"

"'Yes ma'am," they both replied in a contrite manner. "Good night."

Mom looked over at Dad and said, "Hmm – maybe I should make them watch more snake-cult movies."

Dad just shook his head and grinned.

A MIRACLE

On a converted hospital ship near the west coast, Amber's father consulted with a team of doctors to determine whether she was ready to be transferred to a local hospital for further treatment. She rested in a bed quarantined away from other specialists and passengers. There, thankfully, a ventilator and other devices were nearby. Amber was practically comatose, and her pulse weak. Her grief-stricken father spoke to her, hoping for a response.

"Amber honey, can you hear me?" he asked. "Move your index finger on your right hand if you can hear me."

Amber showed no response - the doctors nearby shook their heads. She might be their next fatality. Her father continued on and cried, "Speak to me baby, anything."

A doctor approached him and said, "It's no use. She just isn't ready to be moved at this time."

But as Amber's father finally decided to leave the room, he stopped and turned, facing her.

"Amber," he murmured, "before I forget, there was a boy who called for you yesterday, a 'Ripp', I think, 'Ripley Kovid.' Do you know him?"

It was at that precise moment Amber's heart monitor went off the chart – "BEEP BEEP BEEP BEEP" – and it grew even stronger as her eyes opened for the first time in days.

The doctors and Amber's father were shocked and overjoyed at the sudden change.

The amazed doctors consulted with each other once more. Then one of them walked over to deliver the news of their decision to Amber's father.

"We can't say what happened or how it happened, but we're certain she is ready to be moved now," he said.

CHAPTER FOUR

BACK IN THE SADDLE

The next morning, Mom and Dad Kovid arrived at the local hospital to pick up Grandpa and were first in line to check in at the main desk, which was 'manned' by a female hospital employee and a police officer.

"Good morning! How may I help you?" asked the desk receptionist.

"We are here to bring my wife's father home," Dad replied.

"His name?" she asked.

"Raymond Brudd," Dad replied.

"And your name?" she inquired.

Speaking as quickly and as low as possible, but still understandable to the human ear, Dad replied "Rod Kovid."

The hospital desk receptionist's job required long hours and a calm demeanor, but after many frantic days of dealing with the Wuhan virus, she really didn't have a sense of humor intact anymore. "Right," she coldly responded. "And your REAL name?"

"Kovid," replied Dad. "K O V I - "

The attending police officer stood up and looked Dad in the eye. "Alright sir," he ordered, "I need you to step aside – " Mom quickly rifled through her purse, took her driver's license out, and showed it to the officer.

"There," she said.

The Police officer still stared at Dad while slowly taking the license from Mom's fingertips. "You have GOT to be kidding me!" he guffawed. "Well, sorry about that!"

He smiled sheepishly at Mom and Dad, then kindly lamented about the cruel coincidence, saying "I really feel embarrassed for you guys, same sounding name as the epidemic and all."

"You're welcome," replied Dad, as Mom frowned at his use of sarcasm.

The hospital desk receptionist attempted to brighten things back up by smiling as if nothing had happened, and said "Ok, well, if you will both take a seat in the lobby, we will bring out Mr. Brudd, momentarily."

As the Kovids walked back to the lobby, Dad remarked to Mom, "I am all for changing our last name, because of this kind of reaction."

"What if it had been named Brudd's Disease?" she asked.

Dad just groaned at her little witticism as they sat down.

A few minutes later, Grandpa was wheeled out to the lobby wearing a mask.

"Dad!" cried Mom Kovid.

"Hey Pops!" said Dad Kovid.

Grandpa replied in as clear a voice as he could muster, "Please get me out of here."

But his new friend, Nurse Nancy, followed him nearby and confronted him.

"You mean you've tired of me already?" she asked. "What happened to our karaoke session?"

"YOU are always welcome to stop by. In FACT, I need something to write with - a pen, paper, anything!" he replied.

Nancy just happened to have a pen and note pad, and handed them over to the old man, who performed a rapid scribble on the pad and handed it and the pen back to her.

"Here you are, gal," he said. "Hand this out to all of your friends and keep a copy for yourself."

Nurse Nancy looked at the writing to make sure it was legible, and then replied, "See you soon, hopefully NOT here, though."

"See ya," he shouted, as she walked away.

When the three Kovid family members were outside of the hospital, Mom looked at her father and asked, "What was THAT all about?"

Grandpa looked at her quizzically. "What was all what was about? Ohhh, HER. We became fairly good buddies back there. No hanky panky, though," he answered with a smile, while winking at Dad.

"Righht," replied Dad, winking back at him.

Mom stopped to raise her eyebrow at him, then they continued on to the car. Just as they exited the hospital grounds, Amber was brought in by ambulance, followed by news reporters. Her father soon arrived, and the reporters flocked to him.

REPORTER # 1:

"Sir, is it true your teen daughter experienced a miracle while aboard the hospital ship?"

AMBER'S FATHER:

"No comment."

REPORTER # 2:

"What was the nature of the miracle? Was it an angel?"

AMBER'S FATHER:

"No comment."

REPORTER # 3:

"What is your daughter's name?"

REPORTER # 4 TO REPORTER # 3:

"Amber. It's Amber."

REPORTER # 3:

"Sir, what is YOUR name, at least?"

AMBER'S FATHER:

"I am Amber's father."

No further comments were allowed as the hospital guards and employees blocked the reporters from entering the building.

TV NEWS PERSONALITY:

"Well, as you can see, Amber's father is reluctant to share the nature of her so-called miracle, causing this station to wonder if it is all a hoax made up by the Pres - "

CLICK

"I've seen and heard enough of this hinkum dinkum," said Tom *the International* as he set the channel changer aside. "Miracles, mish mosh. Reg! Where are my goodies and get-well letters?"

A HINKUM DINKUM MIRACLE

"Coming, Tom!" cried Reg.

Tom looked at his watch, then strode over to Reg and said, "I am losing faith in you, mister. How can you ever expect to be considered good enough to marry my cousin, Spanka, if you cannot even follow the slightest direction?"

"Spanka?" asked Reg.

"You know who I mean, my cousin Rati!" yelled Tom. "Spanka is her childhood nickname."

Reg felt somewhat sad for the girl, and asked, "Doesn't Rati have a say in this matter?"

Tom puffed himself up and replied, "No . . . not even if she THINKS she does. Now get the car. We are leaving today."

Reg also felt somewhat downcast having been pushed onto poor Rati instead of just being allowed to date her, normally. As he exited the room, Nurse Nancy entered.

"Well, are you looking forward to going home today?" she asked.

Tom gave her a big, insincere smile as she checked his vitals, but in doing so, she thoughtlessly left Grandpa's phone number and address out where Tom could read and copy it.

Nurse Nancy used a stethoscope as well as a sphygmomanometer in these cases, as electronic devices, no matter how well designed, had their flaws. "Everything looks good, so I think you are ready to be checked out of here. I believe you have a ride ready?" she asked.

"Oh YES ma'am," he replied, acting as if he were to receive a lollipop for being good.

"We'll need your signature, then you're ready to go." she said. But as Nurse Nancy left the room, his ingratiating smile morphed into a sinister grin.

THE MOMMA FACTOR

As Grandpa arrived home with Mom and Dad from the hospital, Ray and Ryk stood on the front porch to greet him. They apologized for their part in the karaoke debacle, and he readily accepted it. Then as he walked inside and sat down on the couch, the boys filled him in on all news since his illness. It is at this time Ripp turned the TV on while the rest of the boys spoke with Grandpa.

TV NEWSCASTER:

"Our reporter on the scene earlier at the hospital spoke with Amber's father, but not exactly receiving any feedback. Jim?"

NEWSCASTER JIM:

"Seems it will be awhile before we find out how a girl on the downswing with COVID-19 made such a remarkable U-turn to recovery. Meanwhile in celebrity news . . ."

Ripp quickly turned the TV off and begs Ray to drive him to the hospital.

"Ripp man," spoke Ray in compassionate mode, sitting down beside his besotted brother and placing an arm around him, "Amber is in ISO-LATION! At least she should be, and you SHOULDN'T be anywhere NEAR her, yet!"

Ripp replied "I don't CARE what happens - I need to see her!"

Mom had heard enough, noting Ray couldn't get through to him with kindness and sensitivity.

"How's this, then - FORBIDDEN? Now, find something constructive to do," she commanded.

Ripp stormed off to his room, leaving Ray and Ryk to shake their heads. His obsession with Amber was going to do him and others around him some real misery if not dealt with soon.

TOUCHÉ AND WELCOME BACK

The next day, Ripp, having been denied being driven the hospital, was alone at home when the bell rang. The postman was at the door with a large package delivery, COD, addressed to the Kovid boys. Ripp paid for it, even though there was no return address. Taking it to his room and opening it, he thought the old karaoke system must've been replaced through a warranty. Within minutes he was singing songs. Lots of them; sad, lonely love ballads.

About seven hours later at dinner call, he showed up at the dining room entry way, looking pale and weak.

"'I don't feel so good," he groaned, and passed out.

The family looked on worried as Grandpa, Ryk and Ray looked to each other - they've seen this before.

"I'll get the car," said Dad.

CHAPTER FIVE

BAD PENNY REPRISE

Back at the hospital, Mom and Dad checked in at the main desk, where they dealt with the "Kovid" vs "COVID" thing, but were spared interrogation through the intervention of the jovial police officer who met them at the time of Grandpa's illness. Dad agreed to stay with Ripp while Mom returned home to confront the guilty. She and the two boys, Ray and Ryk, joined by Grandpa, try to put the pieces together of how Ripp managed to inherit the non-Corona virus Grandpa suffered.

With hands behind her back, Mom paced up and down the line of three like a military officer surveying the troops.

"Now," she began, "I would like to ask all of you, but mainly Ray and Ryk, how has this device come back into our lives?"

"Dunno mom, we just found it in Ripp's bedroom," Ryk replied.

Ray jumped into his little brother's defense and adds, "Ryk and I went to a store to try and donate it."

"You tried to DONATE a filth-laden karaoke set? WHERE? And HOW did it manage to find its way back under our roof?" she demanded.

Grandpa knew the boys were talking their way before the firing squad and spoke up, saying, "Maybe I should explain."

"Please do," answered Mom, now her back to them.

Grandpa continues, "My roommate at the hospital is a foreign kid who has the same virus as myself, and he managed to get it, he said, from a karaoke machine that smells like the main river of his native country."

Mom turned around and asked, "Now let's see: Ray and Ryk DONATED this stinking foul device . . . "

"Ah wait, Mom - he didn't accept it, and he ordered us to throw it away into the dumpster in the back of his building," said Ray.

"And did you?" she asked.

"Well, that's just it mom," said Ryk. "Ray left it in FRONT of the dumpster."

Ray stared at Ryk for ratting on him.

Mom looked at Ray and stepped in front of him.

"Ray?" she asked.

Ray replied, "Mom, the guy was dishonest and obnoxious. WE, Ryk and myself, waited around to see if he would take it, which it seems he did."

Then Ray turned and whispered to Ryk, "Big mouth."

"Hey!" the surprised Ryk replied to his big brother.

Mom continued on, "Then this contraption manages to find its way back to square one. Can anyone here explain this COD delivery receipt I found on the floor?"

Ray and Ryk shrugged their shoulders.

Mom looked over to her father and asked, "Dad - is there ANY possibility our address got into that boy's hands?"

"Not from me," he replied. "My IDs were with you the entire time."

"What about the note you handed to that nurse?" she asked.

Ray and Ryk looked at each other somewhat confused, but after it had dawned on them what their mother was talking about, they smiled at their grandfather, and he returned their smiles with a wink.

"Way to go, Grandpa!" declared Ray.

"Oooo! Woof woof woof!" grunted Ryk.

"Thank you, boys," replied the old man.

"Weasel Mae Crowbait, eat your heart out!" Ryk cried.

Grandpa and Ray looked at Ryk, trying to decipher what his utterance meant.

"DAD - focus!" shouted Mom.

Grandpa remembered the original question and with his hand on his chin, thought aloud.

"Maybe the little fella found the note by accident. He WAS suppose-ed to leave the same day as me, after all. Nancy probably dropped the darn thing, and he managed to pick it up. Good eye."

Ray and Ryk looked at him, and together replied, "Nancy?"

Their grandfather smiled with pride and answered "Yeah."

The boys patted him on the back, threw playful punches, horsing around until they heard their mother yell, "Dad!"

"Oh yes," he remembered. "I apologize. Of course, I apologize. You boys should too! This is your mother talking to you. You should respect her wishes and do what she tells you to do the next time."

Ray and Ryk knew the routine. "Sorry MOM - LOVE YOU," they replied.

However, Mom had seen this routine before, and wasn't fooled.

"Yeah right, now get RID of that thing, and I mean PROPERLY! Burn it, trash it, bury it, but remove it, and NOW." She demanded.

"Yes mom, LOVE YOU," they reiterated.

Their mother pointed to the door.

Grandpa stood beside her and said, "You boys heard your ma, now skedaddle!"

Mom squinted over at her father in distrust and said, "You go with them."

Grandpa grumbled as Mom turned the TV on, and began to mumble "Aw, h – " when he was cut off by a cheerful TV personality.

CHEERFUL TV PERSONALITY:

"HELLO, everyone out there in COVID-19 quarantine land, and welcome to the morning wind up! Well, today – "

Suddenly the telephone rang.

Mom turned the TV's volume down to answer the call.

"Kov -you know, residence, uh, hi." She said.

A male voice replied, "Hello, this is Amber's father. May I speak with Ripley please?"

A CUNNING SCHEME BEGINS

Grandpa, Ray and Ryk sat in Ray's car for half an hour trying to come up with a grand farewell to the karaoke machine. After a few bad plots--some daring, but unworkable--the senior of the demolition-slash-exile crew went back to a simpler proven method.

"There's a trick I learned in the service. Let's see if it still works," said Grandpa.

Ryk was ready for anything exciting and asked, "How dangerous is it?"

"Not dangerous," Grandpa replied, "just smoke and mirrors. Maybe our friend, Tom, will finally learn his lesson."

"I doubt it," said Ray. "He will get more cunning. Why don't we just have a bonfire and be done with it?"

Grandpa rebuked Ray's otherwise good plan, saying, "Because we're under a quarantine order. No can do."

Ryk agreed with his grandfather, adding, "Yeah Ray, listen to Grandpa. So, what do we need to do, GP?"

THE POWER OF SONG

Ripp, meanwhile, was kept overnight at the hospital for observation, but he felt alert, didn't have very much appetite, but seemed a bit better. Dad, who was still at the hospital, received a call earlier from Mom, and had a surprise for his son. He checked the time in order to make his exit without any alarms going off from his unsuspecting middle offspring.

Dad thought for a second, then said "Hey Ripp, I'm going out for some coffee, and will probably be back in about an hour. Mind answering the phone while I'm gone?"

"Sure Dad," said Ripp. "Not much happening around this place anyway."

"Great," replied Dad. "Thanks. It might be a loved one."

"Ok, Dad," Ripp answered.

Dad walked out of the room grinning ear-to-ear. A few moments later, the phone rang.

Ripp wasn't in much of a mood to speak with anyone, but he decided to soldier his way through it. "Hello?" he asked.

A female voice over the phone replied, "Ripp?"

"Mom?" he asked.

The voice on the phone laughed and said, "Mom? This isn't mom, silly - it's Amber!"

Ripp was so overjoyed at that moment, he couldn't say anything.

But Amber heard something odd from Ripp's end of the line, and she asked, "Are you crying?"

"No," he replied at first, but then quickly confessed, "Yes."

Amber thought his response to hearing her voice was cute, and she confessed with tears, "Glad to hear your voice, too."

They shared thoughts, laughed, spoke disparagingly of hospital rooms, and talked of getting together soon.

Dad joyfully listened from the doorway and decided it was time for another cup of coffee and then home.

OLD SCHOOL CINEMA

Mom and Dad Kovid had experienced a very long day. Putting two kids and Grandpa in line, then Ripp's situation brightened up by Amber. They decide to hit the hay early. Ray and Ryk, sans supervision, decide to check out obscure and dubious cable movie selections.

"Here's one," said Ryk. "Shubah Dubah Holiday."

"What's it about?" asked Ray.

Ryk began to read: "Three classmates from some unpronounceable country try to outdo each other in a fishing celebration by – "

"No thanks," Ray replied. "What else?"

"Let's see," continued Ryk. "***Paddle Cakes, aka Bird Kernels Ahoy!*** Hungry, downed airmen on a raft in the Pacific try to sunbake seagulls after swatting them down with a paddle. That's kernels with a 'K' and not Colonels with a 'C'."

"Next," Ray answered.

Ryk seemed a bit more enthused about the next title, as he exclaimed: "*Let 'Em Have It!*"

Ray came alive, inquiring, "What's THAT about?"

"The aftermath of a battle at sea, starring Lars Woombuge and Sassmile Froop," Ryk replied.

"Yeah?" Ray asked.

"Yeah," concurred Ryk. "Furious combatants meet once more when members of a sunken enemy ship attempt to hitch a ride with the same US Frigate they previously targeted for destruction. Not Rated."

Ray didn't take the bait either. "What's with all this aqua stuff?" he asked. "How about something NOT water-oriented?"

Ryk kept reading through, suddenly stopping and mentioning another possibility: "Ok. Ah - here we go - '*Dolapoo!*' starring Noobie Jay Score. Classic 'sploitation movie from the early seventies."

Ray sighed and said, "Go for it. Gotta be better than '*Paddle Cakes*' at least."

Ryk changed the channel to a rarely seen afterhours cable selection. The brothers sat back while slow funk music played, the scene being a street from a 1972 night in the hood.

A man wearing an orange fedora, long orange fuzzy single-breasted coat, wide cuffed bell bottoms and platform stack shoes is greeted like a hero by all as he makes his way to his apartment.

A few hours later, there is a break in at the apartment.

They hear low, single bass notes, a wood block and a rattle-type rhythm instrument, while at the same time, the camera follows three hoodlums: one wearing a dew rag and a wool lined buckskin coat, the second one wearing a turtle neck sweater and ski jacket, the third sporting a two-foot wide afro, has gold front teeth and wearing a leather jacket.

The criminals check their weapons while marveling at the white shag carpeting on the wall, featuring a crushed velvet portrait of the owner with two female dancers and a white dog. They nod their heads to his taste in ladies and pets, then continue on, quickly finding a cabinet drawer that has a golden hair dryer, gold scissors and a gold electric trimmer all on a stylish belt. They are so involved in the drawer contents, they fail to notice the orange, robed figure behind them wearing fuzzy orange platform slippers.

ORANGE ROBED FIGURE SPEAKING WITH A DEEP RICH VOICE:

"Unless you know how to use those things, I would put them back."

One of the hoodlums turns the hall light on by mistake. The music crescendos with trumpets.

AFRO HOODLUM:

"What're you supposed to be? And to think I was almost scared."

DEWRAG HOODLUM:

"Yeah blood, he ain't nobody - you tough guy, huh? Fluffy orange stacks man. Rightttt."

The robed man hands the afro hoodlum his business card. The one thug who CAN read does read it to the hoodlums, causing them all to guffaw and "kee kee kee" hiss to the point of irritation.

AFRO HOODLUM:

"So, this your pad, brother?"

ORANGE ROBED FIGURE:

"It is."

SKI JACKET HOODLUM:

"So, this name of yours from the card. What, you inspect septic tanks or clean toilets in that fancy outfit?"

AFRO HOODLUM:

"You just gave me an idea brother - what say we all watch him at work, starting with his FACE?"

DEWRAG HOODLUM:

"I gotcha, man! You sayin' we shove his soft little face into . . . "

Thanks to bad edited-for-TV sound technique, a female voice over-rides the original line ending to: "This DARLING punch bowl!"

Ryk and Ray looked at each other while laughing.

"WHAT???" they both cried in unison.

"Quiet in there," yelled Dad.

The two brothers tried to keep it down, but this movie didn't seem to allow for that.

ROBED MAN:

"C'mon and TRY it baby, if you think the three of you bad cats can handle this weak little toilet cleaner."

AFRO HOODLUM:

"Well, ain't you done gone and akst for it? Go get him, 'G,' and don't take all three seconds."

The Dewragged hoodlum named, 'G,' goes after the robed man, gets grabbed by the ear and seat of the pants instead, then goes flying out of the window as a short wailing scream is heard.

AFRO HOODLUM:

"Hey man, you done gone and killed my bro 'G,' - now you gotta DIE! Go get him, Doc!"

The crying Afro hoodlum points to the ski jacket hoodlum, who whips out and flips a switchblade.

SKI JACKET HOODLUM:

"C'mere, dog boy, I needs to show you sumpthin."

Doc, the ski jacket hoodlum, attempts to square off with the robed figure, who performs an incredibly lame-looking side kick that flips the knife into ski-jacket's forehead and impales the hoodlum on a hall light at the same time.

"Aahh!" gasped the Kovid boys, trying to keep it down.

The afro hoodlum is now sweating from fear but doesn't back off.

AFRO HOODLUM:

"Now you REALLY gone and done it, man - prepare yourself for KUNG FU thirty EIGHT!"

He pulls out a long, silver sound-muzzled pistol.

ROBED FIGURE:

"We need to remove some of this excess material first."

AFRO HOODLUM:

"Whaa – "

The robed figure performs a lame-looking, but loud-on-contact, swishing roundhouse kick, knocking the long gun out of the hoodlum's hand. Then he places the afro hoodlum in a headlock while plugging in the gold electric hair trimmer at the same time.

ROBED FIGURE:

"Let's check out some of this treasure you little boys found tonight."

He starts trimming the man's afro hairdo.

AFRO HOODLUM:

"Hey man, HEY MAN! Dat's my FRO!"

ROBED FIGURE:

"Hold on now blood, I'm almost through."

The robed figure has finished trimming the hoodlum's afro into a large figure 'D.'

The hoodlum struggles as he is body-locked by the robed man.

HOODLUM:

"Hey SUCKA - I ain't yo dawg!"

ROBED FIGURE:

"Thanks brother - I almost forgot – "

The Robed figure grabs some perfume, a flea collar, and two tiny pink bows. The hoodlum gets sprayed, ear-bowed, and collared.

ROBED FIGURE:

"All done - now if I was you, I'd get to walking, you mangy mutt!"

The hoodlum gets booted out the apartment door whining and squealing.

ROBED FIGURE:

"And, remember, that's for FREE - you tell those other mangy street mutts not to mess with . . . "

The apartment scene fades, as a chalk figure of a man comes into view from the vantage point of the platform shoes to a very distant broad-brimmed hat. Then the title appears, as a woman's voice says over street funk music:

"Dolapoo!"

Ray and Ryk by this point, are practically rolling on the floor over this insane cinematic time capsule. Meanwhile, Dad listened to the all too familiar music, and immediately got a bad feeling. Mom had her own suspicion.

"What is that perverse racket coming from the living room?" she asked.

Dad looked around nonchalantly, and replied "I don't know, but it reminds me of something I saw at a frat house or drive in."

Mom looked him in the eyes and inquired "What? When? Where?"

The thing for Dad to do at this moment was to not waste one hour on interrogation.

"I'll go see what they're up to," he answered, and swiftly headed for the living room.

But Mom wasn't quite finished.

"A DRIVE -IN, Rodney? A DRIVE-IN?" she shouted.

Dad arrived in the living room and ordered the boys to turn the TV set off.

"Don't worry Dad," said Ray. "It's been edited for TV."

"Yeah Dad - it sucks, but in a good way," agreed Ryk.

"Oh yeah?" asked Dad. "We'll just see."

He then sat down beside his two-thirds brood.

As the funk music plays, Dolapoo is seen driving through the inner-city in a huge, shag-carpeted Cadillac. He stops, gets out of his car, walks using a diamond cane, and wears the same orange street outfit from the day before, fedora, fuzzy jacket, bells, and stacks.

In other words, he appears to be a pimp.

With much fanfare and respect from the citizenry, he enters a dog salon. Removing his hat and coat, changing to comfortable shoes, and putting on a white smock, he then greets his first client of the day, a miniature poodle.

DOLAPOO:

"Well aren't you a sweet little thing? Come on up here for Uncle Dolapoo and let me help you look purty."

Then the movie came to a commercial break.

"Well, this is certainly not what I had expected," said Dad.

"I know, right?" Ray replied. "At first I thought it was a . . ."

Then he caught himself and stopped.

"A what?" asked Dad.

Ray continued carefully, saying "Really bad movie, but it's, you know, interesting."

"Hmm," replied Dad.

"Hey, the movie is back on!" cried Ryk. "Shh!"

A female wearing a long black leather coat, stiletto heels and a black leather bandanna with floppy ears attached strolls into the salon while walking a black Labrador retriever on a leash.

RECEPTIONIST:

"Hello, how may we help you?"

WOMAN WITH LABRADOR:

"I wish to see Dolapoo."

RECEPTIONIST:

"And, whom may I say wishes to speak with him?"

WOMAN WITH LABRADOR:
"Black Lab."

RECEPTIONIST:
"Oh, of course, he is so beautiful."

WOMAN WITH LABRADOR:
"SHE is Samantha. I am Black Lab."

RECEPTIONIST:
"Oh my. Please follow me."
The mysterious woman, Black Lab, is led to Dolapoo.

DOLAPOO:
"And, what may I ask is the reason for this unexpected pleasure?"

BLACK LAB:
"So, you HAVE heard of me."

DOLAPOO:
"This is a small city. Would you like to have a drink somewhere and talk?"

BLACK LAB:
"How about . . . a good, fun, mind-blowing WORKOUT instead?"

DOLAPOO:
"Ooooh yeah, lead ON, baby."

Back in the bedroom, Mom hears what can only be described as "slow, naughty, sleaze funk" music. Then, there are the groans and well-timed soft grunts that caused her to run down the hallway to confront Dad and the boys.

Mom stomped down the hallway to the living room and stared at her guilty bunch.

"WHAT are you three watching?" she demanded.

Dad pointed to the couch for her to sit, and then shushed her.

"How dare you shush – " she began, as the movie appeared.

Dolapoo and Black Lab are in the gym wearing fuzzy orange and black leather sweats, respectively, and using the rowing machines.

BLACK LAB:

"Whew - that was a good long workout!"

DOLAPOO:

"I can do this all week-long baby. Now, how about some lunch?"

A commercial break begins.

Mom stared at the screen and then back to the males of the house.

"I know," said Dad. "It's not what I expected either!"

"Yeah Mom, it's been edited for TV!" added Ryk.

Mom was relieved and said to Dad, "Scoot over."

"Sure," replied Dad.

"So, let me get the plot straight," queried Mom. "Shaft has a poodle salon?"

"Yeah, crazy, huh?" answered Dad.

Mom was still a bit dubious of Dad's former drive-in history and in a thinly covered warning said, "You're not out of the doghouse yet, mister."

The boys moaned "Ooooh . . . "

"It wasn't meant to be a pun," she said.

"Oh," they replied.

"Movie," said Dad.

"Shhhh," they all warned each other, simultaneously.

Black Lab and Dolapoo are now in a swanky restaurant, one that allows pets for some reason. Suddenly, Black Lab straightens up when a sinister-looking figure appears at the door with a big dog beside him.

DOLAPOO:

"What's wrong, baby?"

BLACK LAB (WHISPERING):

"My ex - he's out of jail!"

DOLAPOO:

"What's his name?"

Right at that moment, a very ugly man wearing a neat Homburg, loud tie and double-breasted overcoat approaches their table with his large dog.

BLACK LAB:

"Shanky Brown."

SHANKY BROWN:

"Where you been, baby? I been looking all over town for you!"

BLACK LAB:

"I had business."

SHANKY BROWN:

"I see. Well, let me introduce myself to your soon-to-be-completed business."

He looks down at Dolapoo and introduces himself.

SHANKY BROWN:

"Hello business, I am – "

DOLAPOO:

"Rottweiler."

BLACK LAB:

"His dog's name is Jezebel."

DOLAPOO:

"I was referring to HIM."

Shanky Brown is surprised to hear his former nickname from a stranger.

SHANKY BROWN:

"Have we met before?"

DOLAPOO:

"It's a small city."

Mom, meanwhile, was busy pondering the theme of this 'gangsters with pets' film and finally asked to any who were listening, "This is kind of an inner-city dogsploitation film, isn't it?"

Ray replied, "Very little mayhem, but a lot of pet grooming."

Dad understood her script dilemma, mentioning "I can see why the genre didn't take. Ah, well . . . shall we?"

He then stood up and proffered his arm to his wife.

"We shall," she replied. "Don't stay up all night waiting for another gangster's dog to appear. G'night, boys."

She then strolled arm-in-arm with her husband to their bedroom, woofing and howling.

"Ugh - makes you wonder at what point adults stop acting normal," noted Ryk.

Ray put his arm on his little brother's shoulder and said "Ryk, you're well on your way."

END OF A LONG DAY

At the hospital, Ripp slept peacefully, still holding the phone after a long conversation with Amber.

Back at home, Grandpa was snoring away, holding his cell phone after falling asleep talking with Nancy.

Mom and Dad are snoozing at last.

Ryk and Ray continued their pillow fight between scenes from the long-forgotten seventies flick "Dolapoo!" and couldn't wait for the next "so-bad-its-great" movie on the same channel.

CHAPTER SiX

QUESTIONS, QUESTIONS

The Kovid family was at home, watching and listening to the President of the United States holding a press conference in the Rose Garden. Some of the younger liberal female press are attempting to play pseudo-question, verbal protest volleyball with him. It starts with one reporter trying to control the microphone with insult, innuendo and crocodile tears, causing the President to select another hand-waving member of the female press corps, who in return attempts to yield her question time BACK to the original reporter. The President has had enough of this election year sensitivity session, and shuts the show down early, waves to everyone present, then turns and walks away. Weeks of psychological material has written itself for his detractors.

"Well now," said Grandpa, "THAT should show those whiny press brats a thing or two. Maybe they'll show a little respect from now on."

"Or as little as possible," replied Mom. "And on THAT subject, dad, what did you three decide about the disease box? Is it gone, as I asked? Removed, destroyed, erased, detached from the surly bonds of our – "

"I get it," said Grandpa, cutting his daughter off in mid-diatribe. "It seems to me that we did. As I recollect – "

THE CUNNING SCHEME

One day earlier, Grandpa, Ray and Ryk were planning a way to deal once and for all with Tom *the International*. Grandpa's scheme seems a bit outdated, and not to mention, cruel.

"Grandpa, I believe Shanghaiing is actually illegal in the United States," Ray pointed out.

Grandpa disagreed, and using an old example, replied, "Well, I think the French Foreign Legion would be the best thing for him. Give him a fresh start and a new name. That 'Tom' business just doesn't fit the foreigner."

"'Pierre' doesn't go very well either," said Ryk. "He doesn't look like a Frenchman, anyway."

"How do you expect to get him there, anyway?" Ray asked.

Grandpa continued on, "Just find a trawler heading out to Morocco, or a tramp steamer to Europe. We throw a few bucks to somebody to take him off our hands, and everybody's happy."

"I hope you're kidding," said Ray. "You ARE kidding, aren't you, Grandpa?"

Ryk agreed with Ray, and asked, "Yeah, where are WE gonna find that kinda dough anyway, GP?"

Grandpa laughed and said, "Of course I'm just kidding. Tramp steamer? Haven't seen one of those since I was a kid. Besides, that feller would just take over the ship in no time. Born leader, he is."

Ray was in complete agreement with his grandfather, even stating "Probably voted *Most Likely To Be Strangled By His Own Employees* in whatever kind of school he attended in his old country."

Ryk's mind lay in the quickest method. "Why can't we just dump the karaoke set in his yard?" he asked.

"Or send it COD to his parents overseas?" Ray inquired.

"I dunno, let me think," answered Grandpa. "We don't know where he lives or where he's from."

"You don't think he has a girlfriend, do you?" asked Ryk.

"Who in her right mind would put up with HIM?" mentioned Ray.

"Boys," said Grandpa, "the best thing is to take the loss, and dump this crate. It has been interesting, and it has put some folks to the test, but now it is time to part ways with it for good. I want to go home with a clear conscience."

Ray thought about this, and put forth a solution: "What say we go find a dumpster?"

Grandpa smiled and said, "Now that's using your head, son."

"What about the one we tried to use the first time?" offered Ryk.

Grandpa and Ray simultaneously shouted "NO!"

"All right," said Ryk. "Just asking."

Grandpa looked on the side of the road and asked, "Hold on son, is that a dumpster over there?"

"You mean that one near the park?" inquired Ray.

"There's always construction going on over there," said Ryk.

Ray remembered when he was a kid and the place was nothing but trees. "Yeah, it will all be houses where the trees are now," he stated sadly.

Grandpa did not care much about that just then. "Pull over there," he ordered.

"Are you sure? There?" asked Ray.

"Yes – THERE!" barked Grandpa.

"You tell 'im, GP!" laughed Ryk.

"I will, and I did," replied the old man. "Good boy. Now let me try to get out of this . . . well HECK, what am I saying? One of YOU young badgers hop out of this jalopy and toss that thing to its forever home!"

Ray spoke up, saying "That means YOU, Ryk."

"Go get 'em, tiger!" yelled Grandpa.

Then in a low voice he said to Ray, "Good display of work detail, son - definitely living up to your namesake's standards."

"Thanks, Grandpa Ray," replied his namesake.

"Don't mention it," said Grandpa.

When Ryk got back to the car, Grandpa asked, "Git 'er done?"

"I stuck it on top of the heap. Don't think nobody will care." Answered Ryk.

"Don't think ANYONE will care," mentioned Ray.

Grandpa grinned and proclaimed, "That's my namesake!"

"While I do all the grunt work," muttered Ryk.

"You are our feet on the ground," declared Grandpa.

"And, always appreciated," commented Ray.

"Good work, soldier," said Grandpa.

"Or marine," insisted Ray.

"Oh yeah, them too," affirmed Grandpa.

"Oh yeah?" Ryk responded. "What if I prefer to be treated like the Coast Guard, instead?"

"Get ready to test a LOT of life preservers," stated Ray.

Grandpa added just ONE bit of sagely advice for his youngest grandson: "Summer's a-comin, fishbait."

"Oh boy," thought Ryk.

TYING UP LOOSE ENDS

After Grandpa completed his entire karaoke narrative to Mom, the next subject of interest came up.

"Well, I hope that ends this chapter," said Mom. "We certainly cannot afford to keep family members up at the local hospital hotel for one more night. Speaking of which – "

"'I am on my way to wrangle our middle son home, mama," Dad replied.

"Then why are you still here?" she asked.

THE POINT SYSTEM

Back in the local hospital, Ripp was in his room and in conference with Amber's father.

"So, you are saying that I am allowed to see Amber once she is well?" Ripp asked.

"Ripley," replied Amber's father, "It is about that sensitive subject wherein we need to come to a certain understanding. Ground rules if you will."

"Ok," Ripp responded.

Amber's father started out by giving some sensitive background. "Young Master Kovid," he said, "I lost Amber's mother a few years ago, and my daughter is all I have to remember her by. To me, she is gold. My precious diamond. A rare and beautiful flower. And Ripley?"

"Yes sir?" Ripp asked.

Amber's father continued, "I am a man with a treasure I intend to guard with my life. And now, YOU are drawing very near to my treasure. And, I intend to trust you by testing you with the care of that treasure. Do you understand me?"

"Is this a pirate thing?" Ripp wished to know.

Amber's father replied, "It is a trust thing."

"Yes sir," answered Ripp.

At this point, Amber's father paced slowly around the room, like a great general before the battle.

"He reminds me of my mother," thought Ripp.

"So here is how it will happen," stated Amber's father. "I will have you on a point system, or demerit system, if you will."

"How does it go?" asked Ripp.

"I will TELL you how it goes. You will start with a score of one hundred, a full merit count," Amber's father replied.

"Ok. Thank you, sir," said Ripp.

"THEN, for every infraction made, there is a demerit count, and it will cost you a specific number of points. If you slip below a score of eighty-five, it is over. No questions, you will be out of her life. Understood?" Amber's father asked.

"What exactly are the infractions?" asked Ripp.

"I was coming to that," was his reply. "One demerit or point subtracted from your total score for hand-holding until she is seventeen. One demerit or point subtracted for being out with her after eight pm on a school night. One demerit or point subtracted for sitting too close together anywhere."

Ripp pondered this and asked, "But what if we go out to a movie?"

"You will have a chaperone, and you will pay for her. Dutch if she asked you out to a movie," Amber's father replied.

"Yes sir. Is that all?" inquired Ripp.

"That is NOT all," Amber's father replied. "TEN points or demerits for being in any bedroom alone with her. Sixteen points and dismissal for kissing, sixteen points and dismissal if you lie to me. This is all on your honor. I will meet with you once a week to see where we stand. And, you WILL be scored for appearance and there is immediate dismissal for any cursing."

This was all too much for the boy. Before he met Amber, his biggest problems were jerks and algebra.

"What about telephone or cell phone privileges?" asked Ripp, fearing the answer beforehand.

"Thank you Master Kovid, I almost forgot," mentioned Amber's father. "No calls after eight pm, no calls while I am out, and ESPECIALLY no loaded words like 'love', 'baby', or any other amorous terms until you are at least twenty-one. Are there any questions?"

Ripp felt the weight of the world on his shoulders and it was all because of a classmate.

"No sir, I guess not," Ripp replied.

"Then welcome to our family and have a respectfully wonderful time with Amber, as long as you remember and stick to our rules of the guarded treasure, also to be known as the Code of Conduct. We will, in time, talk about your future. I believe that the armed services are a great way to start," Amber's father concluded.

Amber's father bid Ripp good health and proceeded to exit the room. Dad Kovid appeared shortly afterward to drive Ripp home.

"Morning, Ripp! How're you feeling?" his father asked.

"I think I just volunteered my way into military dating school," Ripp replied.

"Say what? Can't be THAT terrible," said Dad.

"I would dare speak the sad lament of one exceedingly misguided youth taken in by the deleterious cares of this world while we drive home," spoke the lovelorn lad.

Dad was stunned by Ripp's poetic outburst of lament, but very proud at the same time.

"Hard to believe it's my middle son coming up with this stuff. Ray I would believe, but my hard-nosed sixteen-year-old? Speak on, oh sage of love and remorse," his father replied.

"That's one demerit, dad," declared Ripp.

"Already?" decried Dad. "And I was just getting to know your mother so well . . . "

THE NEW KOVID CUSTOM

The family greeted Ripp at the door of the house, as several unmasked neighbors amble by on the sidewalk

This quarantine will never be the same.

HELLO, MY BUDDY, OR ONE MORE MIRACLE

At the local park, an international meritorious society intended to honor those sons and daughters who have managed to create a life for themselves in town while also serving their fellow countrymen and women during the quarantine. The speaker of the group asked one of his stage handlers how they were able to rent a sound system on such short notice.

The stagehand whispered to the speaker, "It was a miracle - we were going crazy trying to find something, a place that had sound systems today, and there this thing was!"

The speaker whispered to the stagehand in reply, "Ah, good."

Then the speaker turned to the distanced and bemasked audience: "Hello friends, and blessings! Before we begin the festivities, let us greet a family member who has stood out all year long as an instrument of good will. Daman, would you please come up and join me onstage?"

Daman, aka Tom *the International*, walked up to the stage in all false humility and pretend love for his fellow countrymen, saying "Thank you, greetings and blessings."

"Daman," requested the speaker, "please tell everybody what you have been doing for the last year to make others like us feel welcome."

Daman grinned like a Cheshire cat and proceeded to bloviate about his simple hardworking life: "Greetings and blessings, dear brothers and sisters. Well, I – " he began, when suddenly, he noticed for the first-time, what system he was speaking on. He looked over at the stagehand and growled in a low voice, "Where in Kish Nishim did you find this thing?"

The stagehand smiled and whispered back, "It was like a miracle - I found it on top of the trash dumpster!"

Then he gave Daman two thumbs up.

Daman turned beet red, then being able to contain his rancorous temper no longer, yelled and cursed as the startled speaker began the festivities early.

CHAPTER SEVEN

A MOST WELCOME VISITOR

Back at the Kovid residence, Mom and Dad were listening to Ripp's rendition of his first formal meeting with Amber's father. It seemed to them the rules of dating engagement were tough, especially for a free-spirited sixteen-year-old. The only thing to do at this point was to invite Amber and her father over for lunch ASAP and try to work out an easier-to-follow method of teen control. Mom performed the task of dealing with Amber's father, and after some attempt at banter, a decision was made.

"So how did it go?" asked Dad.

"'That man,'" stated Mom, "seriously, I think he belongs in the World Health Organization, if he doesn't already. I invited both he and Amber over, and he asked how many people would be here. I answered 'all of us'. He stated he will allow Amber to visit, since you and I are home, but he thinks too many people are gathered together here in one place without masks or proper distancing."

Dad thought it over and said, "Well, at least we get to finally meet the world-famous Amber. Is she really as cute as some people say, boys?"

"She is even cuter, dad," confided Ray. "How Ripp managed to get her attention, I haven't a clue."

Ryk blurted out, "He is the perfect boy toy for her, that's how."

"Ryk!" protested Mom.

Ray stood up at this point and attempted to bring clarity and calm pertaining to his little brother's outburst.

"What Ryk is trying to say, Mom, is that Ripp is not only sweet and forgiving, he is also pliable," he reasoned.

"Yeah, Mom," assured Ryk, "Ripp is one of us good-looking Kovid boys, only he's a pushover and a wuss."

Ripp happened to enter the room after the insults had subsided.

"I heard my name. What's up?" he asked.

"Your baby doll sweetheart is coming over for a visit," confided Ryk.

Ripp was still too overwhelmed with rules to deal with Ryk's moments, replying, "Don't say it that way, it's a demerit. Mom, is this true?"

Mom reassured Ripp by way of a mild overview. "We wanted to meet your friend and her father, only he won't be joining us."

"Still too good for the lowly Kovid family," chided Dad.

"That's his tough luck," retorted Ryk. "More for us."

Mom needed everyone to be focused and that meant knocking off the jokes and stories. "She will be here soon, so let's clean up," she urged. "Make the place presentable at least."

"Why don't we just show her how we really live?" asked Ryk.

Mom looked at Ryk and replied, "Because you will be the first one sent to a foster home once someone figures out that a family actually attempted to raise children in this squalor."

"Wouldn't 'squalid hovel' be a better way of putting it?" argued Ray.

"Just clean it up," said Mom. "She will be here soon."

Ryk sided up to Ripp and murmured, "Honey baby sweetheart!"

"Shut up, Ryk," warned Ripp.

Ryk then made smooching sounds, forcing Ripp to pillow-pummel him.

MISS CORONAVIRUS USA OR - AN AMBERIC VISITATION

Amber arrived at the Kovid home to the greeting of Ripp's entire family awaiting her at the front door. She wasn't just striking in looks, she was quite the personable presence disguised as a five-foot four-inch cheerleader. The two boys, Ryk and Ray, were dumbfounded, incapable of communication. Mom, Dad and Ripp were the only people who could function normally in the girl's presence.

Mom took her by the hand and said, "Please come in. I'm Ann, the mother of these three otherwise normal boys."

Amber smiled and replied, "Pleased to meet you."

Dad upstaged his wife, momentarily, to mention, "I'm Rod Kovid, father to the same."

"Hi. I'm Amber, of course," the girl replied.

"Of course," concurred Mom and Dad.

As they all entered into the dining room, Amber was seated next to Mom and across from Ripp. Dad was at the head of the table. Ryk was seated across from Mom, and between Ripp and Ray.

Meanwhile, Ryk and Ray tried their best NOT to stare at their visitor. Mom introduced the two dumbstruck brothers to the lovely young lady.

Amber looked across the table, wishing to find out more about the youngest brother.

"Ryk?" she asked.

The youngest Kovid family member looked up from the table quite startled, and gasped "Aah! Uh, Hi."

Amber used a bit of inquiry: "I've seen you around the school with Rip a few times, but what grade are you in?"

Ryk lowered his voice to sound older and replied, "I am in the seventh grade."

Amber lowered her voice as well and mimicked him, saying, "Well OK." Then she smiled at Ryk, which caused him to turn beet red.

During the abnormally quiet time, Dad was dying to ask the girl one question, and now was the moment.

"Amber," started Dad, "what does your father do for a living?"

But right at that very moment, her cell phone rang. Amber excused herself, and answered the call in the living room.

Mom whispering to her husband, "Not now, Rod."

"But how about the timing of that call?" he replied.

Ray looked over at Ryk and whispered, "She sure rocked your twisted little world, huh, bro?"

Ripp took that statement as a cue to perform a closed-eye smooch-face at Ryk.

"Hey!" whispered Ryk, harshly.

Mom shushed the boys as Amber returned to the table.

"Hospital checking up on me," Amber confessed, and she apologized for the interruption.

The boys just stayed silent.

Amber looking around, and asked, "What's wrong?"

Mom, being the official spokesperson, cleared it up for her.

"They're still in shock at having an actual teenage girl in the same room with them," she admitted.

Amber took this information in stride and came up with an idea.

"Well maybe we should have a belching contest after lunch, right, Ray and Ryk?" she offered.

Both boys were stunned, having been caught off guard by the sweet little prankster, while Ripp was practically rolling on the floor.

"Ripp told me everything," she confessed.

"They sure took the boredom out of THIS quarantine," admitted Dad.

Mom, being ever vigilant, politely suggested watching a nice TV movie, instead.

They all agreed, and as a group, quickly ambled over to the freshly-cleaned living room.

MÚSICA PARA MINHA AMADA

This was the one time in the history of the family Kovid that two females took charge of the movie selection. The males of the house winced as a whole when the title, The Karmee Maravilha Story appeared, but they behaved, didn't moan, and most importantly, pretended to be interested, especially after getting 'the look' from Mom.

INTRO

There is heard schmaltzy Latin music and the sight of mountains, an ocean harbor, beautiful birds in the air and trees as a field full of Brazilian kids play soccer. An old singing papaya salesman on the street suddenly loses his voice, and a little girl named, Karmee, who saw him from the soccer field, runs up to him while trying to hold onto her funny homemade hat.

KARMEE:

"What is wrong, Senhor Joao?" (Pronounced 'Zsho-wow' or 'Joe-ow.')

JOAO:

"I lost my voice, Karmee. If I cannot sing, I cannot sell. It is that simple."

KARMEE:

"May I try?"

JOAO:

"You know anything about mamão? Of course, you do, you're Brasilian! Give it a try!"

KARMEE:

"Sim, Senhor Joao."
(singing)
"Mamão for saale . . . mouth-watering mamão . . . for SAAAALE."
. . .

(The boys from the soccer field run and search to find boxes to play samba, joining Karmee.)

KARMEE:

"Mamão!"

SOCCER BOYS (REPEATING):

"Mamão!"

KARMEE:

"For sale."

SOCCER BOYS:

"Mamão!"

KARMEE:

"Come and get some sweet mamão for sale!"

SOCCER BOYS:

"Mamão."

NARRATOR:

"Karmee repeated this multiple times, then found herself dancing a Samba and singing the same song over and over. Joao rubbed his chin, dramatically, and pointed his finger to the air."

JOAO

"I have it - come with me, menina . . . "

NARRATOR:

He took Karmee by the hand, and the boys followed. Joao introduced her to the local restaurant owner, who is floored by their sales song, and so he hired Karmee and the boys to provide music for the restaurant after that.

Now we see her a few years later. The restaurant owner took her to see a cousin who used to work at the Arca Dance Hall and Restaurant in Rio de Janeiro.

KARMEE:

"Do you think I am good enough?"

COUSIN:

"You are more than good enough - someday you are going to be known as . . . "

(Scene changes to the Arca stage.)

ANNOUNCER:

"The sensational Karmee Maravilha!"

(A Carnival-dressed Karmee and the grownup boys, now men, perform samba music.)

Finally, there was a commercial break.

Amber was in ecstasy, exclaiming, "Samba is FUN! Those old songs were incredible."

Mom felt free for once to actually express thoughts to one of her own kind and replied, "They WERE. And how about her headdress?"

"Delectable!" cried Amber. "And those stack-shoes! Her dance moves really enhanced the simplicity of the tunes."

The men of the house were silent, shocked to hear Mom actually sound happy.

"I hate to admit it," said Ray, "but you guys are right. Off the hook, as the old folks used to say."

Ryk still couldn't figure out the 'elephant' in the film. "What's up with that banana hat?" he asked.

"She needed to eat between songs," confided Dad.

"Ah," replied Ryk.

Mom didn't bother to straighten Ryk out about the real reason for the performer's exotic headwear, saying, "Shh . . . it's back on."

NARRATOR:

Broadway show producer Sam Wentwold entered the Arca for a diversion. He obtained a seat near the stage, and experienced Karmee for the first time.

SAM WENTWOLD:

"By gosh, she's a female Al Jarson!"

KARMEE:

"Tiki tiki tiki tiki BOOM chika BOOM . . . "

SAM WENTWOLD (grabbing a nearby waiter and shouting):

"Get me a telephone!"

WAITER:

"O que?"

SAM WENTWOLD (making telephone gestures to the waiter while barking out loud):

"Telephono, por favor!"

WAITER:

"Ah, sim!"

(Snapping his fingers, signaling to the bar.)

NARRATOR:

"So Karmee Maravilha was on her way to New York, just in time for the World's Fair. But she quickly took control with her style and tunes, causing all of New York City's show-going public to take notice."

KARMEE: (singing)

"Meu coração"

BAND: (singing)

"Meu coração"

KARMEE:

"Meu coração esta agradecida!' Chicki chicki BOOM chicki BOOM!"

(The crowd goes wild.)

NARRATOR:

"After a few years onstage wowing the theater world and being forced to take English lessons, Karmee began a crossover into show tunes. But Sam Wentwold realized the real money was in movies, and therefore, sold her contract. Karmee was now on her way to Holly-wood, and under contract to Max Callousey, head of Jaded Pictures."

MAX CALLOUSEY:

"So, who's dis new skoit I gotta deal wit?"

VP OF JADED PICTURES:

"Karmee Maravilha, the Brazilian Sensation!"

MAX CALLOUSEY:

"She some kinda Spanish entah-tainah?"

VP OF JADED PICTURES:

"She is a South American Latina, but not – "

MAX CALLOUSEY:

"She is now officially Spanish. Bringah in."

VP OF JADED PICTURES:

"Do come right in, Miss Maravilha!"

MAX CALLOUSEY:

"My dear lady, please haves a seat! So, you're da Latin sensation, is dat correcto?"

KARMEE:

"Correctiva. I am probably the ONLY samba singer from Brazil to become popular in America."

MAX CALLOUSEY:

"Nevah hoid a dah place. So, from now on, you're Spanish. And if I gets lonely, I'll give ya a call, ok? Now yas can go."

KARMEE:

"But . . . "

VP OF JADED PICTURES:

"Thank you, Miss Maravilha. You will be hearing from us soon."
(She walks slowly out of the office.)

VP OF JADED PICTURES:

"So, what do you think, Max?"

MAX CALLOUSEY:

"What does I TINK? She's shoit, her talkin' voice is too high--like its coming offa typewritah--and she looks a little too built for comfort. We needs tah crank a lotta pictures outta dat senorita, so ticky-tacky, high-pitched, and cuddly ain't gonna cut it. What is dat stuff we advise for stretchin' folks beyond dere normal capacipicities?"

VP OF JADED PICTURES:

"Amphet –"

MAX CALLOUSEY:

"Ah - I don't needs tah know, just do it. And den dere is dat voice a hers."

VP OF JADED PICTURES:

"Cigarettes?"

MAX CALLOUSEY:

"Yeah, dat'll bring down her tone. Dats all. Git on wit it. Oh yeah, one more ting - find some whiny weasel actor tah marry her who'll push her buttons da way we wants. Make a big production of it, bring in mariachi bands, dat kinda stuff. The public loves an exotic weddin."

(The VP nods his head and leaves.)

NARRATOR:

"As time went on, Karmee starred in such films as Road to Uruguay, Time for Tanks, Bombers and Bombshells, and the Spanish American Review."

KARMEE (singing):

"I yi yi yi yi yi love you VEDDY much . . . "

NARRATOR:

"Then there was her war bond drive . . . "

KARMEE (SINGING):

"Pardon me Joe, is that the Mexicali Choo-Choo?"

NARRATOR:

"But every once and a while, she would mix Portuguese and English to please her audience, and to play down the dangers of studio treatment to foreign actresses."

Ray looked around the room at this point and interjected, "Her songs also got progressively worse, anyone else notice this?"

"Show tunes were the disco of their day," noted Dad.

Mom also took this time to shush them, causing Amber to stifle a giggle.

NARRATOR:

"Karmee stunned her biggest critics with a lyric-speed performance record in the otherwise unheralded cinema flop, The Poofy Prince."

(Dark stage, then we hear . . .)

KARMEE (SLOWLY SINGING):

"Amphetamina . . ."

(The curtains rise, and the stage lights are on Karmee. The rhythm changes to quick samba in 4/4 that feels like 2/2, with four-bar guitar lead in.)

KARMEE:

"Once upon a time they call-a me Big JumBoo, because I like to eat papaya and feijoada too, then I was a Hollywood menina, and I take amphetamina, now no one gonna call-a me a Big JumBoo!"

MALE SINGERS:

"Once upon a time they call-a her-a Big JumBoo, cause she like-a eat papaya all the day, but now she take amphetamina, and she look-a lot-a leaner, and-a no one dare to say to her, You Big JumBoo!"

KARMEE:

"Coconut and cola nut and cafe too, with a creamy leche and sugar all the way, and a dreamy cake to stay awake, and frutas too, no wonder they all say to me, You Big JumBoo!"

"Once upon a time they call-a me You Big JumBoo, because I like-a eat-a rice and a barbeque, but now I take amphetaminee to look-a nice and skeeny, so no one gonna call-a me a Big JumBoo!"

MALE SINGERS:

"No one gonna call-a her a Big JumBoo, cause she take amphetaminas all the day, now she always get-a thinner, and she look-a like-a winner, and most of all she's not a look-a like-a Big JumBoo!"

KARMEE:

"Just because my hair is falling, and I hear the angels calling, my amphetaminas they no take away, cause I am-a so much leaner and I always get-a meaner, when I think that I was once a Big JumBoo!"

"Once upon a time they call-a me Big JumBoo, because I like-a lay around and sleep all day, but now I take amphetameepee, and I never feel-a sleepy, and most of all I'll never be a Big JumBoo!"

MALE SINGERS:

"No one gonna call-a her a Big JumBoo, cause she take amphetaminas all the day, now she never feel-a sleepy, and all the food look kinda creepy, and most of all she not a look-a Big JumBoo!"

(Two-bar guitar solo exit, applause and commercial.)

Ripp enjoyed the rhythmic tune, but needed to ask to any who could answer, "What is JumBoo?"

"I think it means 'jumbo,'" replied Amber. "Gosh, I wonder if I should take amphetamines?"

Ripp, Ray, Ryk and Dad all answered her swiftly with a resounding "NO!"

Amber blushed from the response in the room and replied, "Thank you."

Mom was a bit disturbed at Dad's attention to Amber, and whispered to him, "We need to talk."

"I just got caught up in the moment," he whispered to her.

"Is that what that was?" she asked.

"Of course, dear," he replied. "You, on the other hand may consume as many amphetamines as you wish. Grrrr . . . "

"Hmmph," snorted Mom. "Don't bet on it. Call me a 'Big JumBoo,' but I like my lazy papaya eating ways."

Amber's cell phone rang again.

"Hello?" she asked. "Oh, hi dad. Ripley? Yes, He's right here. Ripp, it's my dad."

"Hello sir," said Ripp. "What are we doing? We're watching an old movie about a Brazilian drug addict."

"S I N G E R," whispered Amber.

Ripp corrected himself, "Singer, I mean singer. So how close am I sitting to Amber? About a foot and a half away."

Amber's father replied, "That is one demerit. And Amber is not to know anything about our agreement."

Then he hung up.

"What was that about, son?" asked Dad.

"He just wanted to know how we were doing," replied Ripp.

"Well, Amber, try and bring him along next time," offered Mom.

Amber replied, "I will try, Mrs. Kovid."

"Ann," corrected Mom.

"'Ann," repeated Amber.

The movie was back on.

NARRATOR:

"Over time, Karmee's fame waned, and American show tunes weren't helping her back to the top. So, she went on to star in television, that new medium. But after many years of cigarettes, alcohol and amphetamines, her final performance showed America what a real trooper she was."

KARMEE (BACKSTAGE):

"I don't feel so hot. Can't breathe well."

SHOW HOST:

"You wanna cancel? See a doc?"

KARMEE:

"Nah. I'll get better. Just can't seem to catch my wind."

SHOW ANNOUNCER:

"Karmee Maravilha!"

Karmee (dancing samba and singing):

"Tico tico tico tico."

SHOW HOST:

"Waits a minute dere, Karmee . . . let's swing it!"

KARMEE:

"Yeah!"

(Both Karmee and the show host swing dance, when suddenly she collapses.)

SHOW HOST:

"Hold yer hearses! Stops da music!"

(He whispers to Karmee.)

"You ok, kid? Let's get you to da hospital, ok?"

KARMEE:

"No, I will go out the way I began. On stage. But give me . . . "

SHOW HOST:

"Yeah?"

KARMEE:

"Give me . . . "

SHOW HOST:

"Yeah?"

KARMEE:

"A ceegarette!"

SHOW HOST:

"Get this brave gal a tobacco stick, and din go ta commoircial! Pronto!"

(Karmee takes the cigarette, the show host lights it, and she takes a puff.)

KARMEE:

"Farewell world . . . ugh."

(She grabs her chest and dies.)

SHOW ANNOUNCER:

"This show has been brought to you by Oldport cigarettes, the tobacco-eeyest flavor ever!"

SHOW HOST (KNEELING NEXT TO KARMEE):

"Drat - wrong commoicial."

NARRATOR:

"Although Karmee lived a short life, her inspiration is still strong, especially in her old town of Rio, where her spirit will sing free forever!"

(Karmee is seen with wings, flying, and singing over Rio de Janeiro. Many people down on the street are seen in a conga line and singing "I yi yi yi yi yi.")

"She inspired a few interesting folk downtown, that's for sure," said Dad.

"Yeah," observed Ray, "there's this one kid at school who wears makeup and . . ."

"Ahem," grunted Mom.

"Thank you for the movie everyone, it was fun," said Amber.

"Even the weird show tunes?" asked Ripp.

Amber replied, "Especially those weird old show tunes."

"Well, I need to clean up in the kitchen," mentioned Mom, "so if you'll excuse me - "

"Please let me help you," offered Amber.

Mom looked at Ripp, then mouthed the words, "She is a winner" while pointing to Amber as they both exited toward the kitchen.

Ray spoke up and said, "Those old show tunes are painful."

Dad agreed about that, but he also conceded one thing: "Her early stuff was great though."

"Yeah," admitted Ripp, "that movie studio really trashed her out."

The only Kovid male not to opine on the subject was Ryk, who at that time was fast asleep on the floor.

Ripp looked around, and then said to the non-dozing guys, "I think I'll head over to the kitchen."

Ray and Dad gave him a thumbs up.

DISHES, DADS AND DEMERITS

Mom and Amber were in the kitchen washing dishes when Ripp walked in. But just before he could say anything, Amber's cell phone rang. She answered it and handed it over to Ripp.

"It's my dad," she explained, and with a smile returned to drying dishes.

"Yes sir?" replied Ripp.

"Ripley, I am on my way over. Did Amber have a wonderful SAFE time?" he asked.

"Yes sir," Ripp replied.

Right about that moment, Amber and Ann started to sing "I yi yi yi yi yi love you VEDDY much!"

Amber's father asked, "Is that Amber singing?"

"Yes sir," said Ripp.

Amber's father asked, "Who is she looking at while she sings those words?"

Just at that second in time, Amber looked over to Ripp while singing, then returned to drying dishes.

"Ah, that would be ME, sir," the boy confessed.

"That's another demerit," her father maintained. "You're down to ninety-eight. I'll be over soon to take her home. And Ripley?"

"Yes sir?" he asked.

"Keep your mind on what you need to be doing," suggested her father.

Then he hung up.

Amber was excited, but curious about all of this new banter between the men in her life.

"So, what did Dad say, Ripp?" she asked.

But before the boy could speak, Grandpa rushed into the kitchen from the basement bearing bad news:

The old man looked up and blurted out, "Nancy is sick!"

CHAPTER EiGHT

SECRETS LEARNED

Mom, Amber and Ripp were in the kitchen still staring at Grandpa after his announcement about Nancy the nurse.

"Sick with WHAT, dad?" his daughter asked.

Grandpa looked down at his shoes, then looked up again and replied, "We don't know yet. But she works in that hospital day and night, who knows what she managed to pick up."

At this point Grandpa noticed Amber. "And who is this young lady?" he wished to know.

Ripp brought her before him and proudly announced, "Grandpa, this is Amber."

"Well howdy!" declared the old man. "Heard about ya. Pleased to make your acquaintance."

"Likewise - pleased to meet YOU too," she affirmed. "Very famous about town karaoke lover, I hear."

Grandpa laughed, finally having met a non-related young person darn near to his ilk, "I can tell you and I are gonna get along just FINE," he proclaimed.

"She is already family here," said Mom, as the two ladies smiled at one another.

Amber looked at the clock, and said, "Oh boy, speaking of that, I need to contact my father."

She then exited the kitchen to make her call.

Grandpa watched the girl leave the room, and then said to Ripp, "You sure know how to pick 'em, son. Lovely young gal."

Dad had just entered the kitchen and had heard Grandpa's appraisal of Amber.

"We think so," he said in agreement. "Now, what was all that rushing around about? Hey, that reminds me of a song. Around about, round a - "

"Nancy is ill," Mom stated. "How long has it been since you've seen her, dad?"

Grandpa thought back a few weeks or more, then he replied, "Since I was incarcerated at the local hospital where she works. Little safety feature we added to our friendship. At least until this Wuhan thing has died down."

"Smart move," Dad concurred.

"And lucky for us," agreed Mom.

Amber reentered the kitchen holding her cell phone and announced, "My dad will be here soon. Thanks for having me over. It was a lot of fun, and very nice to meet you all. Ripp, my dad wants to speak with you again."

She hugged him and handed him her cell phone.

Amber took his parents aside and confessed, "I think my father really likes him. He always wants to speak with him."

Ripp reluctantly put the cell phone to his ear and replied, "Sir?"

Amber's father began, "Ripley, I am glad to see you managed to get her home before eight o'clock, and that's good."

"Yes sir," answered Ripp.

Amber's father continued: "Has she said goodbye to you yet?"

"She said goodbye to most of us in the kitchen," acknowledged Ripp.

"Good," the man replied. "Did she hug anyone?"

"Yes sir," Ripp confirmed.

Amber's father then asked, "Whom did she hug, Ripley?"

"Uh, me, sir," sighed Ripp.

"That is another demerit. If I were you, I'd straighten up my act, and fast," warned the man.

Ripp quickly realized something about the rules and countered "Yes sir, but a hug isn't an infract - "

But Amber's father had hung up.

Amber heard most of the one-sided conversation and confronted Ripp.

"Infraction? What do you mean infraction, Ripley?" she demanded.

"Nothing. Nothing," he answered demurely.

"RIPLEY," she demanded once more, sounding just like his mother.

Ripp sadly, but honestly confided to her, "I'm not allowed to say."

Dad stepped in and disclosed to her, "Amber, your father is very protective of you. So Ripp is willing to do whatever it takes to abide by your father's rules."

Then Grandpa chimed in: "Now personally, I'd just be sort of forgetful about those kinds of things."

But Ripp disagreed, and proclaimed, "He's like a super-sleuth, Grandpa. He will find out."

Amber was incredulous. "Hold on, hold on," she insisted. "Rules? Rules for seeing me? You all knew and didn't say anything?"

Mom replied, "We think you are worth protecting."

"Not much leeway," Dad added, "but - "

Amber couldn't believe what she was hearing.

"This is embarrassing," she muttered.

Ripp tried to reason with her, saying, "Amber, I don't mind, especially if it means I can continue to see you."

Dad blurted out, "That's my boy!"

Mom gave Dad a look, then said to her, "Amber, I will speak with him soon, ok? Now don't upset him or even let him know YOU know just yet."

Grandpa added, "Yeah, don't rile 'im up, or you'll both lose."

Amber was inconsolable. "I feel like a royal in all the wrong ways. I don't know who to talk to about this," she confessed.

"Call me whenever you wish," insisted Mom. "I'd love to hear from you. And this thing will work out." She then hugged Amber and whispered, "No demerits for hugs here."

Amber smiled through her tears and thanked her.

Ryk was now fully awake and shouted from the living room, "Amber, your ride is here."

The entire family saw her off at the door. Amber got into her father's car and waved goodbye to them.

Mom then said for all to hear, "That was painful to say the least. Demerits. That poor girl."

Dad agreed, but he also mentioned, "We still didn't find out her father's name. Ripp, what IS her LAST name?"

Ripp suddenly came back to attention and reacted to his father's question. "Her LAST name?" he asked. "Oh, you wouldn't believe it, Dad, what a coincidence."

But right before Ripp could answer, Grandpa called everyone to the living room.

"I think you folks oughta see this," he urged.

DOOMSDAY PREVIEWS

The family watches the live news on TV - A city man recently died in a sickening fashion while in police custody and, now, riots are taking place in many major cities across the country. Police cars are burned, office windows smashed out, stores are looted, and peaceful protesters are shoved out of the way by the violent ones.

Grandpa shook his head and lamented, "Welcome back to nineteen sixty-eight."

Dad was dumbfounded.

"First a virus, now THIS." He concluded.

Grandpa continued, "Nineteen sixty-eight. Some people never learn."

Able to take no more distress for one day, Grandpa headed off to his room.

Ray looked at it logically, but sadly, too.

"I guess there won't be any COVID-19 update today," he muttered in as dry a fashion as possible.

Ryk just stared at the screen as Mom and Dad each placed a hand on his shoulders.

GOOD NEWS, BAD NEWS, CAD NEWS

Grandpa decided to call Nancy to see how she was doing. She actually sounded well, rough, but well.

"How you feelin' gal?" he asked, in as chipper a way as humanly possible.

Nancy replied, "A little worse after watching the news."

Grandpa remained cheerful; though and said, "Yeah, well, seen it before. I suppose we will see it again before long."

Nancy agreed with him, but interjected, "You know what's strange about these protesters?"

"I don't know," said Grandpa. "Tell me."

Nancy told him.

"They seem emboldened by their cell phones," she began. "They walk right up to the police – "

They are now both looking right at what she is talking about on TV--a skinny man wearing a hood, mask, and sunglasses, and carrying a cell phone, rushes up to an officer who is wearing a helmet and carrying a shield. The skinny cell phone-carrying man pushes the officer and then uses his cell phone to record the officer's reaction.

SKINNY MAN:

"C'mon pig, come after me!"

(He tries shoving the officer, but the officer didn't budge.)

"Come on, I dare you, murderer!"

(He shoves the silent officer over and over without reaction while he himself bounces off like an acorn, until the officer slips after accidentally being pushed from behind by one of his own.)

"POLICE BRUTALITY - POLICE BRUTALITY! And you all saw it!"

POLICE OFFICER:

"I slipped. Sorry."

SKINNY MAN:

"VERBAL ASSAULT!"

Meanwhile, another protester limply attempts to break an office window using a lead pipe and eventually succeeds after many tries. He flounces away, while at the same time, recording himself. Soon, many of these protesters are shown gathered together around a burning trash bin, comparing their videos, and bragging about their exploits.

"What a bunch of narcissistic brats," Nancy concluded.

Grandpa remarked in jest, "I still think the French Foreign Legion has a purpose."

Nancy agreed with him, but dismissed the possibility, saying "The problem is getting them shipped there."

"I am all for the fine art of Shanghaiing in this case," proposed Grandpa.

Nancy smiled for the first time all day. "Ah, we get along so well, and we always agree. How long will this honeymoon last?" she wondered aloud.

"For as long as we are breathing," avowed Grandpa. "Now, how's about you changing the channel, and see if you can find some decent entertainment? Beats being alone."

"I'll try," she said. "So, let's see - news, news, news, the zoo, cars, cars, cars, racing cars, a naked man and woman getting sick in the jungle and can't sleep – "

"And a-skeered," Grandpa added.

Nancy liked that. "That's an old one," she agreed. "Yes, a-skeered and a-feared – "

"Change it," said Grandpa. "Those gals are never pretty."

"And how would YOU know?" asked Nancy. "You watch this program, do ya?"

"I am a-skeered and alone myself. Can't help it," replied the old man.

"Uh HUH. Ok - at least you're honest. Oh, here's ONE. Quick - channel, uh, well . . . YOU know, the old-time movie channel!" she insisted.

Grandpa asked, "You mean this old black and white gangster film?"

"Yes," replied Nancy, "that one! The one with Edgar P. Rossington . . ."

"That's him," said Grandpa.

Nancy shushed him, sounding just like his daughter.

"Hmm," he sighed.

TV ANNOUNCER:

"Not since THE PUBLIC ENEMA with James Gagne, THE AFRICAN THING with Humbert Smartcart, or even BAR FACE, featuring Raul Puny has there ever been a performance like Edgar P. Rossington's vicious perfectionist, LITTLE TWEEZER!"

LITTLE TWEEZER:

"I'm gonna give it to ya, and I'm gonna give it to ya GOOD, see . . ."

(They view up close a mobster's face drenched in sweat as a hand comes toward him.)

"Hold still, you mug, it'll all be ovah soon."

(The Mobster yells.)

"Got it! Got that ingrown hair."

MOBSTER:

"Thanks boss."

LITTLE TWEEZER:

"Oh yeah, I GOT it, but you squealed like a little kid."

MOBSTER:

"No, boss - "

LITTLE TWEEZER:

"Yeah, that's right. You SQUEALED. You're a singer, and I don't mean like Al Jarsen."

MOBSTER:

"I can explain —"

LITTLE TWEEZER:

"Explain WHAT? I think it's time you went for a ride. You need a vacation, right? Don't he boys, don't he need a long vacation? GET HIM OUTTA HERE - and don't let me see his face again, at least until next month. And don't forget to send me a postcard this time, you RAT ..."

MOBSTER:

"Thanks boss!"

LITTLE TWEEZER:

"And remember the seashells this time!"

TV ANNOUNCER:

"So much honesty."

LITTLE TWEEZER:

(After removing a tick from his own neck.)
"Ouch! This is it kid, I squealed."

MOBSTER # 2:

"Oh no boss, not YOU!"

LITTLE TWEEZER:

"Yes, me. I gave it to me good, see, and I couldn't handle it. Not tough enough. I couldn't take what I dished out. Now I have ta take me for a last ride."

TV ANNOUNCER:

"So much love . . . "

LITTLE TWEEZER:

"If it weren't for you, I'd a nevah made it - you're the best piece of medical hardware I evah had, and I've had 'em from all ovah the world. C'mere, baby."

TV ANNOUNCER:

"It's Edgar P. Rossington as . . . LITTLE TWEEZER!"

Meanwhile, Grandpa and Nancy were both sound asleep holding telephones in their hands.

THE KID WITH THE GOLDEN GIFT

After the revelation came that she is on a point system, Amber argued with her father in their living room. The news of Ripp's time with her based on a scorecard of demerits was too much, and she headed toward the door.

"Where are you going?" her father asked.

"For a walk or maybe to see Ripp. I don't know," she replied.

"You are not leaving until we talk about this," he ordered.

Amber stood in front of her father and said, "Dad - ENOUGH. You don't trust me or Ripp, who, by the way, is a gentleman."

"He is a boy," her father maintained.

"And so are you, like NOW," she snapped, and walked out of the house.

Amber's father shouted, "Get back in here!"

Ripp, at the same time, was walking toward Amber's house for a short visit, but he forgot to call first. He knew that he was supposed to consult with her father in order to see her without causing anymore demerits. Meanwhile, Amber's father was in the front yard asking her to come back inside as she stood defiantly in the street. What she didn't see was a delivery van coming up from behind her.

Amber's father saw the truck and yelled "AMBER!!!"

Suddenly, there was the sound of screeching brakes as Amber looked around, but before she could see the truck, Ripp came out of nowhere, pushed her out of the way, and took the impact himself.

The shaken driver jumped out of his van, and yelled to Amber's father, "I didn't see either one of them until – "

Amber's father was badly shaken. The thought of losing his daughter twice was too much to handle as he cried out, "Amber! Amber!"

But his daughter slowly rose from the sidewalk with a few scratches and said to him, "I'm ok. What happened?"

The shaken van driver who now stood beside Ripp said to her, "This boy saved you. I couldn't stop in time, I just didn't – "

Amber's father was now back in charge. He looked at the driver and replied, "Call an ambulance!"

Which the driver did.

Then Amber's father went over to Ripp, and called his name, saying "Ripley? Ripp?"

Amber stood over him, caressed his hands and cried, "Ripp! I love you!"

Her father saw this and finally accepted it.

Ripp, who had partially awakened to Amber's voice groaned, "What hap - "

But Amber's father said to him, "Hold on son, help is coming."

As Amber continued to hold his hands, Ripp weakly rebuked her, saying, "That's a demerit."

HEROES AND ZEROES

The next day, Ripp's family, plus Amber and her father, and even Nurse Nancy who was now well, stood by his bedside, wearing masks, of course.

Ripp looked around somewhat confused and asked, "How did I get here?"

Amber spoke first, and said, "You have this interesting habit of saving my life."

But Ripp didn't remember it, and replied, "I did?"

Amber's father, in tears, spoke next and said, "You did, I was there, and I wish there was a way to repay you. Thank you, Ripley."

But Grandpa wasn't letting Amber's father off the hook THAT easy.

"How's about gettin' rid of that point system?" he proposed.

Amber's father smiled and answered, "Done."

Grandpa continued by looking over at Ripp and declaring, "We're awful proud of you, boy."

Dad interjected one small correction, "Young man Ripp, young man."

Ryk crowed, "He's a marine!"

Ray proclaimed, "No, he's a soldier!"

Mom touched Ripp's arm and said, "He's my hero."

"That was MY line!" complained Amber.

Mom placed her arm around Amber and replied, "Oops."

Ripp's nurse entered the room, a bit taken aback by the number of visitors, but just said to them, "He needs his rest now, so you should all say your goodbyes until tomorrow."

Mom and Amber both gave him a hug and a kiss. Amber's father overlooked it with a smile. This time.

On the way out, Dad had Amber's father alone, and now he was finally going to ask him the question he'd been dying to find out the answer to.

"Would you please clear up a mystery for me?" Dad put to Amber's father.

"And what mystery would THAT be?" he inquired.

Dad asked, "WHAT is your NAME? I've been calling you Amber's father this entire time. Who are you? I don't need to know what you DO for a living, but –"

Amber's father smiled at his daughter, then looked back to Rod Kovid and replied, "Sarz. Geoffrey Sarz."

"You're kidding me," said Dad.

Amber's father laughed at Dad's statement of disbelief and said, "With a name like Kovid, you're asking ME that question?"

"Somethin' is tellin' me this could get awful INTERESTING," asserted Grandpa.

Mom was already planning ahead. "I am thinking maybe a green-themed wedding, with masks," she uttered.

Amber's father broke in with, "ONE thing a time, uh . . . "

"Ann," replied Mom.

Amber's father corrected himself. "Ann - besides, this is a teen thing. They could part ways next – "

"DAD," barked Amber.

Amber's father looked over to Ann and said, "Just like her late mother, God bless her."

"Well since we're all here," noted Dad, "what say we do something together?"

"Like what?" asked Mom, suspiciously.

Ryk and Ray broke in with an offer of "Karaoke!"

The remaining Kovids and Amber groaned, "Eeyew."

"What does THAT mean?" asked Amber's father.

"Welcome to the family Geoffrey," said Dad. "The karaoke thing started at the beginning of the quarantine – "

Amber and Mom looked at each other and smiled.

Ryk shuffled over to Ray and whispered, "That Ripp is one lucky sucker."

Ray thought about it and replied, "Yeah, he gets lovesick, then karaoke sick, he had Amber demerits, then he gets hit by a car. Really lucky."

Ryk was not dismayed. "Well," he concluded, "if that's what it takes to keep an Amber, I'm all in."

Amber walked over to him and said, "Thank you, Ryk!"

Ryk told her she was welcome, and added, "Tell all your friends!"

Ray gazed at his little brother with admiration, and opined, "From a punk to a lady's man - this quarantine done you some good, Ryk Kovid."

"HAS done, Ray. The proper format is HAS done," replied Ryk.

As they all headed down the hallway to the exit, Tom *the International* was just leaving the room of another unfortunate karaoke victim. He suddenly recognized the Kovid brothers far down the hallway.

"Is that who I think it is?" he asked. "It IS them! Wait! Police! Somebody stop them!"

But the Hospital security assumed Tom was one among several violent protesters from downtown and they apprehended him.

Tom shouted out, "No, not ME - THEM! They are passing dangerous equipment to citizens! I'll do it myself! You people are so worthless! LET GO OF ME! AAAAArrrrrggghhh!!"

His cursing and yelling faded into the sounds of sirens and ambulances of the latest problems of the hour. His were but a blip in time.

Quarantine time.

A Medieval Latin forty-day period, pronounced phonetically:

Quarantina.

The End

AUTHOR

Wayne Tatum is a walking enthusiast and progressing pilgrim on the rocky narrow road of Christianity who early on experienced life through the perspectives of sports, theater, music, creative writing, and home movies.

He is a self-described class clown who built his voice through self-inflicted wisdom, while honing a comedic discipline that has entertained everyone who has encountered him throughout his up and down lifetime achievements--including church orchestras, blues open mic sessions by way of trombone, and singing.

He is married to a beautiful lady from Rio de Janeiro, and they reside in his home state of Maryland.

CERTIFIED EDITOR

Laurie's writing and editing career is expansive. Her love for the written word, its representation, intent, and accuracy has progressed over time.

Laurie Martin Roberts holds two master's degrees (MSTM and MBA); enjoys buying and selling antiques; creates unique stained glass works of art; and moonlights as an editor for friend's and colleague's published works.

CERTIFICATE *of* EDITORIAL

THIS ACKNOWLEDGES THAT

QUARANTINA

Has been successfully edited for proper English grammar, language, punctuation, spelling, tense, and overall style and delivered to Laughingcleaver Press Imprint, in lieu of Imprint editorial of, "QUARANTINA," prior to "ILLUSTRATED TALES FOR THE EASILY ENTERTAINED. This Certificate of Editorial adheres to terms and conditions of the writer's title representation agreement referencing LOC: 2020943228, which releases, September 2020.

"QUARANTINA," by Mr. Wayne A. Tatum

23 SEPT 2020

Laurie Martin Roberts

SIGNED, *Ms. Laurie Martin Roberts*, Editor.

Laughingcleaver Press

Wayne A. Tatum

APPROVED BY, *Mr. Wayne A. Tatum*, Writer.

SOCIAL MEDIA

FACEBOOK FAN PAGE:
https://www.facebook.com/authorwaynetatum

INSTAGRAM:
https://www.instagram.com/donnainkpublications

LINKEDIN:
https://www.linkedin.com/in/donnainkpublications

PINTEREST:
https://www.pinterest.com/donnaink

PUBLISHER WEBSITE:
https://www.donnaink.com

TUMBLR:
https://www.tumblr.com/blog/donnainkpublications

TWITTER:
https://www.donnaink.com

WORDPRESS:
https://authorwaynetatum.wordpress.com

QUARANTINA

MERCHANDISE

January

Sun	Mon	Tue	Wed	Thu	Fri	Sat
					1 New Year's Day	2
3	4	5	6	7	8	9
10	11	12	13	14	15	16
17	18 Martin Luther King Jr. Day	19	20	21	22	23
24	25	26	27	28	29	30
31						

HAPPY HOLIDAYS
Love the Tatums

HAPPY HOLIDAYS

Wishing you a wonderful holiday season and a joyous New Year.

—

TATUM'S

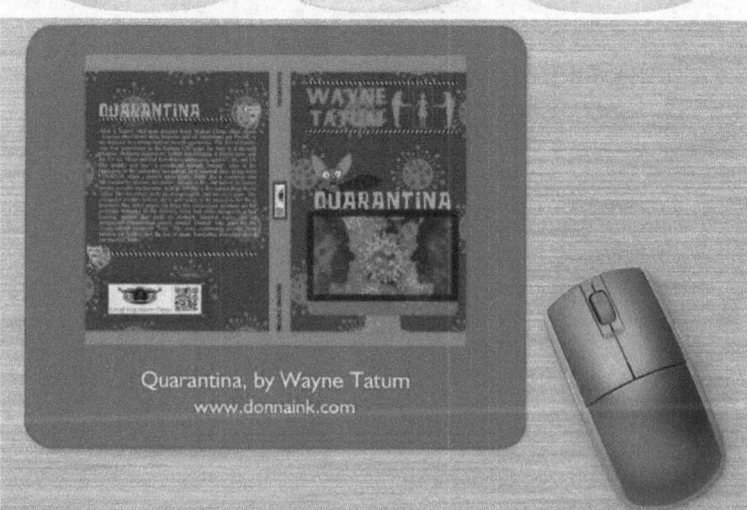

Quarantina, by Wayne Tatum
www.donnaink.com

REFERENCES

Dolamite. Directed by D'Urville Martin, performances by Rudy Ray Moore, D'Urville Martin, Jerry Jones, Lady Reed, Hy Pyke, West Gale, John Kerry, Vainus Rackstraw, Dimension Pictures, 1975.

Down Argentine Way. Directed by Irving Cummings, performances by Don Ameche, Betty Grable, Carmen Miranda (Bambu Bambu), Charlotte Greenwood, J. Carrol Naish, 20th Century Fox, 1940.

Jolson, Al, (The Free Encyclopedia: Al Jolson), Wikipedia, 24 September 2020, https://en.wikipedia.org/wiki/Al_Jolson.

Little Caesar. Directed by Mervyn LeRoy, performances by Edward G. Robinson, Douglas Fairbanks Jr., Glenda Farrell, Warner Brothers Pictures, 1931.

Shaft. Directed by Gordon Parks, performances by Richard Roundtree, Moses Gunn, Charles Cioffi, Metro-Goldwyn-Mayer, 1971.

Laughingcleaver Press

DonnaInk Publications, L.L.C.

Laughingcleaver Press Imprint
DonnaInk Publications, L.L.C.
17611 Aquasco Road
Brandywine, MD 20613
www.donnaink.shop